Conflict Reawakened

By Harlowe Frost

ISBN eBook: 978-1-959981-71-8
ISBN paperback: 978-1-959981-72-5

Editor: Weslee Imrisek
Developmental Editor: Elizabeth Daly
Cover Art: Getcovers.com
Formatting: Huckleberry Rahr

Books In the Magic Of The Galaxy Series

Series 1: Viera Kor

Book 1: Galaxy Lessons

Book 2: Magic Lessons

Book 3: Conflict Lessens

Series 2: Betsy Doeth

Book 4: Conflict Reawakened

Book 5: Magic Rewritten

Book 6: Galaxy Revisted

Acknowledgements

I feel this book was a long time coming. Viera's story ended, and I thought I could be done. Many people disagreed. I decided to continue the story with Betsy, let her continue to tell the adventures of Earth, aliens, and magic. I mean, Viera returned with Thorn to Abritos.

I want to thank Wes Imrisek for taking the time to edit this after it had been "edited". Elizabeth Daly, as always, you are an amazing reader who always makes my stories better. Angela Grimes and Dulaine Roode, you're both such important pieces to my book's development.

As always, I am grateful to all the readers. It is because of you I continue to write and publish my stories.

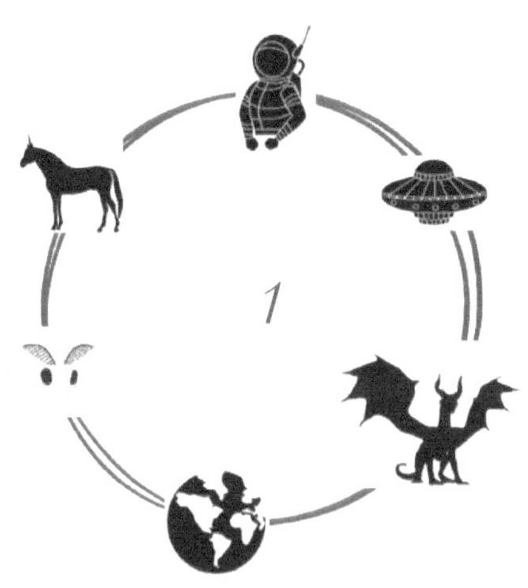

Even an Old Dog Can Learn a New Trick

Betsy

Betsy gazed across the stage at the ever-growing number of people filling the field, waiting for the press conference to start. She rubbed her temples. "I can't believe I'm really going to do this."

Why didn't I convince any of the other Pillars to help?

Her friend Viera laughed. "How long have you and the Pillars been keeping magic and aliens a secret from the people of Earth. Centuries? Longer?"

"If you mean the five of us alive now, then centuries. But if you include our parents, grandparents, and so on." She shook her head. "We always knew this day would come. I just hoped I wouldn't be involved."

Orson, the government official who'd set this all up, smiled wide. "I, for one, am glad to be part of this. Not only do we have you, the most brilliant of all the Pillars, but we also have Viera, the newest magic wielder; Thorn, an amazing alien ambassador; and me. I may be old, but I have some pep to my step yet. Who could ask for a better group?"

A chuckle bubbled out of Betsy as she shook her head. She could think of a few people she'd like to add to the mix, but they didn't have time. They had to get ahead of the misinformation caused by the krottel, those damn alien bugs.

The damn invasion. First, the arrogant bugs open Viera to magic, turning her from an everyday basic human to a wizard. No one knew that was possible before they'd bitten her. Then they'd invaded. And thanks to cell phones and social media, every human on the planet instantly knew about the existence of magic and aliens.

In an effort to save the planet, the damn qynad took to the sky, looking to all who saw them like fire-breathing dragons. They were caught on hundreds of videos, uploaded, and shared.

There was no covering it up. The damage was done. The day they all dreaded was here.

Microphone in hand, Betsy stood center stage, ready to do the exact opposite of what she'd been trained for her whole life.

Am I really telling a crowd of everyday humans about this? We've been trying to keep the knowledge of magic and aliens secret for so long. It hurts my head that today is the day all the rules change.

Betsy took a deep breath and tried to center herself. "Hi, my name is Betsy Doeth. I am what is known as a Pillar on Earth. Currently, there are five

Pillars who have been keeping Earth safe for generations."

My dad is probably rolling in his grave, not to mention Grandpa Gandalf. Our mission for a millennium has been to keep the people of Earth from knowing about magic and aliens until the day we become their teachers. I guess today is that day. "I'll give you more information about what that means later. I'm joined on stage by Viera Kor, Thorn Firoza, and Orson Mard."

Betsy picked out the cameras, speckled throughout the crowd. *Gods above, I better not become a meme.*

She sighed. "We are here to talk to you about what happened the other day all over the planet, but specifically in Chicago, since that is where three of us were." She waved her hand at everyone but Mr. Mard.

"You mean when the aliens and dragons attacked?" someone in the crowd yelled.

Betsy laughed, a smile cutting through her dour thoughts, and smoothed down her shirt. Banter she could handle. "Yes, that's exactly what I'm talking about. Though, you do know you shouldn't believe everything you see on the internet." She waited for the laughter over her comment to die down. "There was an invasion of an alien race on Monday. Despite that, as a planet, we don't need to worry. There is a division of government and specialists that have been working with the aliens for some time. We came together in a joint force to ensure the safety of our world."

There were several shouts of, "I knew it!"

One person in the mass of people yelled, "What makes you so special?"

"I'm glad you asked." Betsy's smile remained plastered on her face, but she still recoiled at revealing these truths. "Each of us has a reason we were part of the team on the ground in Chicago, the main area of the fight. Over the next few weeks and months, we will hold more of these press conferences to give detailed information to all of you. In these sessions, we'll introduce you to the individuals who are part of the team and maybe to some of the alien races who help keep Earth safe. Today, you'll meet the three of us. Mr. Mard is our government contact. He can speak at the end if he wants, but for now, I'd like Ms. Thorn Firoza to give her story."

Thorn stepped up with a wide smile, her beauty a beacon for the crowd to gaze upon. She was in her human form, tall and fit, with flowing auburn hair. The crowd reacted as one would expect: applause, cat-calls, and other cheers of encouragement. Thorn took it in stride.

"Hello, people of Earth!" She waved. "I've always wanted to do that." Her smile grew, intensifying her beauty. "As my friend here said, my name is Thorn Firoza, or as my people say, Commander Firoza. I am from a different planet, Abritos."

Thorn dropped her human image. Her turquoise skin glowed in the morning sun, set off by her dark-purple hair. A stunned silence rolled over the people watching before gasps and small conversations could be heard. This was the first alien many of them had seen in person ... probably any had heard about. The battle had been quick and, for most, just stories and memes.

Thorn continued, "I came to this planet when mine was invaded. Your government let a portion of my people come here as refugees. Our planet has recently been evacuated by its invaders and my people can go home. From the bottom of my heart, we chanzii want to thank you all."

The silence that followed her words was almost deafening. Then, slowly, people shut their mouths, which had been hanging open in shock, and applauded. There were a few skeptical shouts, but Thorn ignored them.

Thorn handed Viera the microphone. "Hi, everyone. My name is Viera … ah, Viera Kor. There isn't a lot special about me. I taught second grade for years." She shot Betsy a glance, and Betsy nodded emphatically. She wanted to say, "You can do it," but they were on stage. Her friend had already been through so much in the last few months, from learning about aliens to having magic foisted on her. Betsy was proud of how far she'd come. She held her smile as she realized how much she'd miss Viera when her friend followed Thorn to Abritos.

Viera's eyes shone as if she could sense some of Betsy's emotions. She turned back to the crowd. "Betsy mentioned there were five Pillars here on Earth. They are wizards, or magic users. I would be the sixth, but I'm heading to Abritos to help them rebuild. I was included in the group of specialists because I am one of only six humans who can wield actual magic."

Viera held up her hands. She created the image of a dragon flying above the crowd. Again, the people seemed to hold their breaths as they watched the display. It morphed into a phoenix, then burst into a ball of fire. The heat could probably be felt by everyone below. A few people gasped, and one shouted in fear.

There was a moment of silence as everyone gaped at her and the magic she'd wielded as if waiting to see what would happen next.

A woman in the middle of the mass of people laughed. It sounded like she wanted to mock them. "You think only six people on Earth can do magic? Arrogant much?"

A fireball flew from the audience straight into the air. The heat emanating from it was like Viera's. Viera seemed about to do something when it exploded into fireworks of pink flower petals that rained over the crowd.

It took a bit of effort for Betsy to sense anything from the crowd. Sensing wasn't her special brand of magic. But what the woman had done was legitimate magic. *What the hell?*

With a grimace, Viera shot a look at Betsy, lowering the microphone from her mouth. "That was magic. I felt the power. You know I'm heading off-planet soon ... looks like you'll have a lot more on your plate than just aliens."

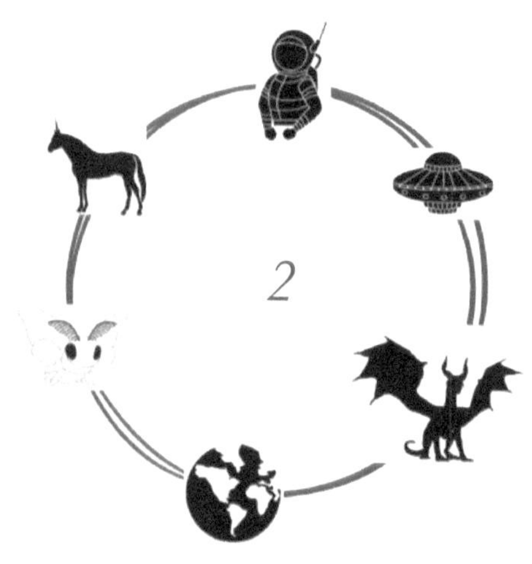

2

The Tip of the Iceberg

Betsy

Just off stage, Betsy rested her head on the tips of her fingers and thumb. The small circular motions on her forehead and just below her eyes didn't help the pounding in her head, but it kept the others from immediately speaking to her.

"We have security gathering the woman who created that display and whomever she arrived with." Orson sounded more amused than frustrated at the magical presentation in the middle of their press conference.

Despite being a top official for the government, he doesn't understand the larger picture in this. The very foundation the Pillars have based thousands of years of Earth history on has shifted under us. Combine that with looking like fools in front of an international audience. For fuck's sake, none of this is good.

She blew out a breath, then plastered on a smile. "Sounds great. Are they taking the group to a conference room? Or are you planning to lock them up for making us international, maybe even intergalactic, laughingstocks?"

Viera snorted, then covered her mouth. "It wasn't that bad. I started off by saying I was new and didn't know much. Lean into that."

Betsy didn't know if she had any smiles left after the big embarrassment, but her friend's willingness to take the blame, and then Thorn wrapping an arm around her and leaning down to give her a quick kiss on the cheek, warmed something within her.

She'd spent years avoiding any sort of relationship. It was near impossible with her longer life. But knowing it was available to others … just like that, she was ready to face the wolves … or magic users … or whatever awaited them.

Orson chuckled. "Arrest them? You're a hoot, Pillar Doeth. You know that, right? Why don't we get to the room ahead of our guests? We can get something to drink, maybe a snack. We'll make sure they know how comfortable and confident we are in this situation."

Viera's face scrunched up. "But … are we those things? Because, personally, I'm confused and a bit cranky."

He laughed and linked his arm through hers. "I'm glad you're going to be our liaison on Abritos, Ms. Kor. You're a delight and quick as a whip."

"I'm your what now?" She leaned away, but he held on tight.

"Oh, don't play coy now. We'll set you up with a way to get communication back to us so you can send quarterly reports. I wouldn't want you out there not able to check-in. How else would you keep in contact with Pillar Doeth and your family?"

Viera's back straightened, and it looked like she grew a whole quarter-inch taller. "I wasn't planning on returning to Earth, Mr. Mard. I am honored by the opportunity you've presented, but I believe I'll be able to find work in line with my training and suitable to my personality on-planet once I arrive."

Betsy bit her lower lip. She knew her friend, but she also knew Orson. He had a way of getting what he wanted.

"Of course you will. I wouldn't expect anything less of you, Ms. Kor. I'm just excited to read your thoughts and impressions of the rebuilding and progress of Abritos. To learn how their society runs would be a boon to help us progress here on Earth, especially since the proverbial cat is out of the bag."

Before Viera could respond, Thorn placed a hand on Viera's lower back. "Before you say 'no,' consider your parents. If half your salary went to them and the other half was converted to Galactic Standard for you, there would be no harm in sending a report every few months. It would be easy."

Amused by the situation, Betsy said, "And, as Orson said, I'd get a copy as well. So, you'd be helping me and the Department of Interstellar Coexistence and Knowledge Sharing."

Viera bent over and covered her face, laughing. Betsy figured it was because of the acronym for the department.

To this day, it was one of Betsy's favorite things she'd named.

They all sat on one side of a cherrywood conference table that could hold sixteen people comfortably. The high-shine table wasn't strictly rectangular. It bowed out on the long sides, giving it an oval feel. On the underside of the antique-looking furniture were well-spaced outlets to plug in several digital devices. There were even some pads for intergalactic electronics. The table was a feat in advanced beauty and function. Betsy wasn't sure how the department secured the item from the dwarves, the only species with the ability to imbue items—a dying magic. It thrilled her to have it.

As they waited for the people from the crowd, Orsen ordered coffee and tea from Miranda Tips, the department secretary. It came just before their guests.

Miranda led the three people in and waved to the opposite side of the table.. Two were young women who looked to be either teens or in their early twenties. The last was an older man, maybe in his thirties. Then again, Betsy looked to be in her thirties and was a few centuries old, so it was hard to tell.

The trio sat across from them, and Betsy looked at the man. He had almost black hair and green eyes. She started with him because he was the oldest of the group and had an air of command. "Welcome. We are part of the group that tends to work with intergalactic relations."

She gazed at each of the two young women. One had golden-brown hair and blue eyes, the other auburn hair and brown eyes. "I—we—are glad you could join us. We'd like to open communication with anyone who has magic. It's something I, and the small group of five we spoke about earlier, have been monitoring for quite a few years."

The woman on the left, the one with the lighter hair, scoffed. "Not very well, I'd guess." She turned to look at her friends and smiled then shrugged.

"Why are we here? What do we have to do with aliens? We're not, you know."

Viera laughed loud enough that the guests turned to her. Thorn and Orson chuckled softly. Viera shook her head. "You're like my students, and that always amuses me in someone older than second grade." She shook her head. "You know exactly why you're here. I can feel your curiosity and interest. You want to see how far you can push us and maybe learn what we can do, but don't want to show your hands too soon." She ended with a shrug. "Now, do you want coffee, tea, or to get to the point?"

"Or some combination?" Thorn added. "You can have something to drink *and* get to the point."

"That's true," Orson agreed. "We're all here to learn from each other. There's no reason for any animosity."

The one who appeared to be the spokesperson scrunched up her face. "My name is Pearl." She hesitated, and then a slight tremor passed through her body. "Just Pearl. You don't really need to know our last names, do you?"

Betsy sighed. She pulled up her phone and texted Miranda. She could do a lot more than basic secretarial duties. She had been with the organization since she was twenty-four and just out of college and, over the last ten years, had proven herself good enough to be an agent. She just didn't have the credentials.

Can you get us the full names of the three people brought in with us?

As she typed her text, Orson smiled at the trio. "Of course not. First names are plenty."

The girl sighed. "Okay. This is Devlin, and that's Cassidy."

The three here are Pearl, Devlin, and Cassidy. The young women look to be in their twenties, and Devlin may be in his thirties. They sound ... southern. Maybe Mississippi or Alabama.

"Lovely." Orson's tone made him seem more like a grandfather and less like someone with a ton of power. "I'm Orson Mard. Next to me is—"

"I'm Betsy, this is Viera, and on the other side of her is Thorn. But you probably know that since we were all introduced on stage."

"Again," Pearl asked, her tone tight, "why were we 'invited' here? Are we under arrest?"

It took a few seconds to unclench her jaw. What Betsy wanted to say was "yes," and then follow through and forget about them. But that wouldn't solve anything. Her phone dinged, and she looked down to see Miranda had texted her back. Suddenly, she felt a lot better about the situation. Miranda was a wonder.

Betsy smiled at the trio. Their reaction made Betsy realize it wasn't one of her nicer smiles. She didn't care, because it made her feel good. She turned to Pearl, the apparent leader of the group, and asked, "Ms. Katz, how old are you?"

Pearl's eyes widened, and Betsy saw all the muscles in her arms and shoulders tense. When she didn't answer, Betsy turned to Devlin. "How about you, Mr. Piedra? Do you have an age?" She turned to Cassidy. "Or you, Ms. Raine?"

Despite Pearl being the one who seemed to lead these three, Devlin was the first to get his tongue moving. "My guess, Betsy—sorry, I don't have your last name at quick access like you do ours—is I'm about your age: thirty-seven. I know it isn't nice to guess a lady's age, but you aren't playing nice, are you?"

A smile split Betsy's face, and next to her, Viera coughed. "Sorry," her friend choked out. "Coffee went down wrong." She made some sounds as if trying to get herself together. Betsy finally shot her a quick glance. She leaned into Thorn, hands over her mouth, eyes wide and tearing. Again, pulling her hands down, she mouthed, "Sorry."

Betsy shook her head and faced the three newcomers again. "No offense taken. Can all three of you do magic, or just the one? And again, are all of you the age you look?"

Pearl's eyes were narrowed. "I'm twenty-two, and Cassidy is twenty-three. I don't know what our ages have to do with anything. Just because I'm the youngest doesn't mean you should dismiss me." She waved toward Orson. "Should I only give him respect because he's the oldest?"

This time, Viera couldn't hold back her giggles. When Betsy looked over, her head was down on her crossed arms and her whole body shook. There was no reason her friend couldn't enjoy herself. The meeting was getting off track.

Betsy rubbed her face. "Okay. I'll answer one of your questions after you answer the one I asked. Do you all have the ability to do magic?"

Cassidy snickered. "Yes, everyone in our town does. Your claim of only six on the planet was ridiculous! You know nothing!" She crossed her arms with a smirk and leaned back.

Pearl groaned. "Cassidy, please. Let me do this. You have officially answered more than she asked. And since she knows our last names, she probably knows where we're from. You did pick that up, right?"

Cassidy's eyes widened. "Um, right. About that drink, do you have soda? I'd love a soda."

Orson stood. "Since I'm very much *not* the oldest in the room, there are two older than me by quite a bit—well, on my side of the table at least—I'll go get the soda. Three? Or do you two want coffee, tea, water?"

Once the others figured out how to work their mouths, they told Orson what they wanted, and he skipped out of the room.

"So." Devlin leaned forward, eyes narrowed. "You're not my age?"

"That's what I'm trying to figure out. If you have magic within you that you're tapping into, it changes you. I'm about ten times older than you."

Thorn shifted into her natural shape. "If you remember from on stage, I'm not from this planet. I don't age the way all of you do. By your counting,

I'm about a hundred and twenty-five years old. My planet's rotation is off from Earth's, so it isn't exact."

Viera had calmed down and sat up. "I just started learning about magic." She shrugged. "Last February, I was like most of the people on Earth and didn't know about any of it. It's a long story, but now I can do magic ... it flows strong within me. So, right now, I'm as old as I look. That said, I'll probably live a pretty long life if the other magical people are to be believed."

Pearl's head tilted as we spoke, then she nodded. "I can call fire. Everyone can." A look of pain crossed her face, then determination. Then she pulled out a small vial. "This is a small potion. Within this bottle, I've created a spell to help me read with clarity." Her face lit up with a smile, and Betsy realized the girl was pretty. "I just graduated college, but I kept these on hand to help with studying. I don't care if it was cheating. Getting a medical degree in four years was what I needed."

"Do you have something like that for turning fire into flowers?" Viera asked, focused on the liquid in the vial.

Cassidy snorted. "That was me. I put my spells in paper. When I rip it, the spell is released. I have some that allow me to transform items into a new shape as it dissipates. I can't do much with the transformations, but flowers are pretty easy."

"Okay, so you imbue your magic into different items?" Betsy's mind hurt. Two witches who casually spoke of a dying proficiency.

"Of course," Pearl said, sounding confused. "Fire and putting spells into things. What else is there?"

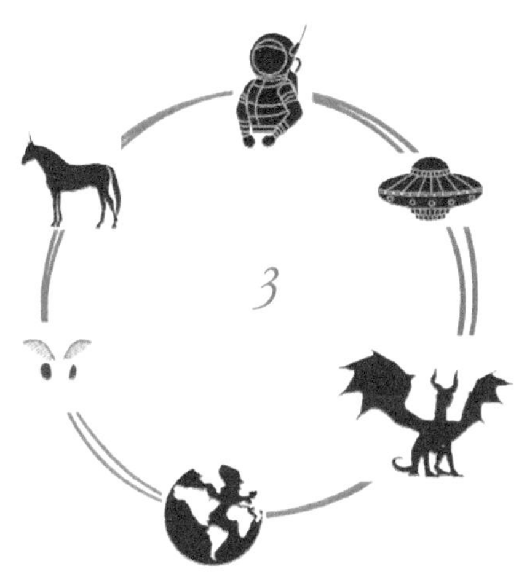

That Awkward Moment When …

Viera

Viera hugged her mug of coffee to her face, smelling the deep, smooth, comforting scent. She sipped a bit. The liquid was almost too hot but was so worth it for the grounding flavor. Coffee was its own spell.

The panel in her kitchen, which now held mugs from the personal collection she'd been given over the years by her students, knew how to prepare the brew perfectly. When she first started using the damn thing Thorn's people had installed, it created a new mug every time. Viera had feared her house would be overrun by the silly black monstrosities.

A small sigh preceded the unclenching of the muscles across her shoulders as she sipped her morning brew, happy with how things had finally worked out.

"Are you really that stressed?" The amusement in Thorn's voice made Viera smile back at her. She looked up from her coffee at the beautiful woman walking into the kitchen and marveled again at how different her life was compared to before spring break.

Then Thorn's amusement tickled Viera's senses. *God, I really need to learn how to control what I pick up from others. I think, if anything, it's getting worse!*

"Yes and no. I haven't seen my parents in over a year ... or three. My life was really different back then." She squeezed her eyes shut, thinking about the last time she'd seen her parents in Chicago when they'd come to the city for a weekend visit. They hadn't wanted to travel *all* the way up to

Wisconsin. Opening her eyes, she sipped the coffee. "I'm not the same person. I don't know if I could even pretend to *be* that person."

For years, Viera, like her parents, lived for each day to be the same as the one before. The best vacation involved her couch, a glass of wine, and a sexy woman renovating a house ... or beating up bad guys in a movie. Then, a few months ago, she'd ended up on a spaceship, heading to a peace summit.

First, she learned there were aliens, and then that Gandalf from all those books and movies was real, as was magic, and then some creepy bug aliens opened up *her* magic.

And although spending her time teaching second graders filled her heart with joy, the idea of relocating to Abritos with Thorn and broadening who she was excited her more. Viera barely recognized the woman she was compared to the person planning that staycation back in March.

Thorn leaned down and gave her a gentle kiss. For a moment, everything slowed and Viera relaxed into the sensations. Once they broke apart, Thorn smirked. "That's better." She walked to the panel and ordered a coffee and two breakfasts. "How long do we have?"

Amusement bubbled in Viera. "Oh, now, this part I like." She thanked Thorn for the plate of pancakes and sausage. "My parents keep asking about what flight we're coming in on and whether I'm *sure* we can afford the last-minute reservation. Father even hinted that, as a teacher, maybe we should've waited until there was some deal on airfare."

"So, they don't watch the news or hang out on social media." Thorn smirked at Viera's wince. "You do know our faces have been plastered everywhere. Memes. They've made memes out of us."

"I don't know what they know, but I'm not going to assume. We'll go, talk, explain, and then have a nice meal ... or not." *They just learned I liked women. I have no idea how this first meeting will go.* "As for the memes, I've avoided looking at any of that. Coffee, no screen time, it's glorious." She shrugged. "Now, my parents ... again, I have no idea. I've lost the ability to understand anything. Five Pillars, a town of imbuing experts. It's all impossible to follow."

Thorn snorted. "Did you see Betsy? I thought her head was going to explode. She usually has such a perfect poker face, but even I could see a reaction from her."

"Do you think it's wrong of me to be leaving tomorrow? Do you think she'll need another person here to help her?"

Thorn slid her hand across the table and clasped Viera's, giving it a squeeze. "No, I really don't. And I'm not just being selfish. She has the other Pillars. She has Orson and the others in that department. But, now that aliens are known, there will be more ambassadors ... more liaisons ... sent here to work openly with Betsy and the others. Don't worry, she won't be alone."

"Do you really think so?" A spark of hope lit within Viera. The idea that a group would help her friend made her feel better about her plans to leave Earth and head to Abritos with Thorn.

"I do. It took a lot to get any of my people to be allowed to live here as refugees on Earth. Our ability to blend was the only reason it was allowed. Liaisons are common throughout the galaxy. The only reason others haven't come is because your government has said 'no.'" There was a twinkle in

Thorn's eyes as she put her plate in the sink. "Well, love, there's no reason to refuse all us aliens now."

Viera wrapped her arms around Thorn's waist, resting her head on the other woman's stomach. "I've always accepted you."

There was a park a block from Viera's parents' house in Gainesville, Florida. Before they transported, Horax, one of Thorn's engineers and a qynad, did a sweep of the area. "Commander, the temperature isn't too hot, but there doesn't seem to be anyone about. I would expect people to be out at a park with nice weather. Could the ship's instruments be faulty?"

"I doubt the computer is wrong, Horax. If the area is empty of people, go ahead and send us." Thorn winked at Viera, her excitement filling the kitchen.

Viera braced herself for the melting sensation of herself and the world around her as she was sent from her house in Madison, Wisconsin, to Florida.

She and Thorn picked up their bags and the house started to disintegrate around them like a Dali watercolor painting. As much as Viera loved the convenience of instant transport, it messed with her mind, even before magic had been opened to her.

Then, trees wavered in front of her, and she was squeezed in by thick, heavy air. For a moment, she wasn't sure she could breathe. She dropped her bag and sweat dappled her skin. *What the hell is this? Are we in some sort of stasis? Did the teleport mess up? I don't know if I can move, much less breathe.*

Next to her, Thorn shook. "Why do people choose to come to this state? To live here? This is awful!"

Demanding air into her lungs, Viera trembled, then forced herself to shift in the thick, humid air, turning her head to look up at Thorn. "So, we're not in some alien trap?"

Thorn barked out a laugh. "No, love, just the natural Floridian welcome."

She'd grown up in Colorado. After she'd graduated from college and moved to Madison, her parents had packed up and relocated here. They'd joked it was where all the old people went to retire, but in reality, they were too young to retire and had quickly found jobs. Several of their friends had moved while Viera had been finishing her education degree at Colorado State in Boulder, and since she'd lived at home the last two years, she figured her parents were just biding their time. Beyond their friends, her parents were probably trying to avoid snow ... something she understood and respected.

Viera spent her summers teaching summer school or volunteering to help in the district. She didn't have a lot of "fun" money after buying a house, so travel had never been in the cards. She always thought she'd spend more than one trip visiting her parents but didn't regret her decision to follow Thorn off-world. The thought excited her too much.

Then a bug bit Viera's leg, and she yelped. Jerking to slap her shin, she picked up her bag and checked her phone for the direction they needed to head. "Before something bigger tries to eat me"—a sideways glance showed her Thorn's smirk—"and not in a good way. Let's get out of here."

The house wasn't far, but they were both drenched in sweat by the time they arrived. When they told Betsy of their plans, she'd snickered and suggested bringing a change of clothes. Viera had assumed it was because everyone in Florida had swimming pools, so they'd also brought suits. Now, she understood the folly of her thinking.

When they got to the door, Viera paused. If they'd been in Boulder, Viera would've just walked in. The house would've been familiar ... her house, the place she'd grown up. But this home was different, unfamiliar. With a sigh, she knocked.

The door swung open and both Viera's parents were there, pulling her into a hug. "Viera!" Mother said, sounding breathless as if she was the one who'd walked through the swampy air. "You made it. And look at you. I can't believe how lovely you look."

"Tammy, let them in. They'll melt. They're not used to our heat ... hell, I'm not used to it. I'm not sure anyone is." Father's gruff voice made Viera smile, and the group entered the cold tundra of the house.

Once the door closed, a small gasp escaped Thorn. "It's really cold in here."

Father mumbled, "Everyone around here keeps their houses like this. You get used to it."

Viera smiled as a shiver ran down her back, then turned to her parents. "Mother, Father, this is Thorn. Thorn, these are my parents, Tammy and Lloyd."

Thorn gave one of her winning smiles and held out her hand. "It's a pleasure to meet you both. I'm honored to be welcomed into your home."

Mother looked delighted. "You are very welcome here. Is there anything you need right away?"

With a sheepish duck of her head, Thorn asked, "Is there a bathroom where we could freshen up? Maybe change out of our sweaty clothes? We brought extra. Someone gave us a heads-up, and she was right. We only walked just over a block, but it's very warm out there."

"Humid ... it's the humidity you have to cut your way through." Father waggled his brows.

"Of course, of course." Mother shook her head, then placed a hand on Thorn's arm, swinging her other arm to the left.

Viera could see a kitchen through the open doorway ahead of them. There was a lot of noise coming from the kitchen. *Who else did they invite?* To the left, where Mother led, was a small hallway that ended in a living room. "Just this way," Mother said, leading them through a living room that held all the furniture Viera remembered from her childhood.

The dining room was part of the great room, separated from the sitting area by a change in flooring. Mother pointed. "Just down that hallway, second door on the right. You'll find us in the kitchen when you're done."

It didn't take them more than a couple of minutes to change. Before they left the bathroom, Thorn embraced Viera. "Just breathe. You're doing great. Just tell them as much as you want. If we need to return, we can. We can get into the whole alien from a different planet thing later if you want." She gave Viera a soft kiss. "It'll be okay."

The tension left Viera's body. "Okay, thank you. I just don't know how much they'll understand. They don't often watch the news and are never on social media. They probably missed most of what happened over the last few days. And if they do know, they don't know the names of who's involved."

Their sticky clothes went in a plastic bag within their pack, and then they headed into the kitchen. It was time to meet the family.

Viera didn't recognize the two women, one blond and one brunette, moving around the large room, cooking. The space was the nicest room she'd seen so far: granite countertops, a large four-burner gas stovetop, and a huge French door refrigerator with a bottom freezer. There was a large island in the center, where her mother sat drinking a mimosa.

Mother stood. "Oh, good, you found us."

Sitting on a stool with a beer, Father snorted. "How could they not with all the noise we're making?"

Mother just waved a hand and motioned them in. "Okay, Viera. You probably don't remember meeting your Aunt Dotty, your dad's sister, but you did when you were very young. As for this other lovely lady, this is Amanda."

Both women had been distracted by their work cooking, chopping, and sautéing. It all smelled amazing.

Amanda was the first to break away. She used the back of her hand to push some of her blond hair back from her face. She stood out, being the only blond in a room of brunettes—well, Thorn had auburn hair, but it looked brunette in the kitchen lighting, and in reality, it was purple. And Father was bald.

Stop going off on tangents!

When Viera focused in on her aunt's ... wife?—*Do I remember them saying they'd gotten married?*—she realized the woman gaped at her and Thorn. "What is it? Did we get a leaf or a squirrel caught in our hair on our way over?"

"It's you!" She spun to Aunt Dotty, who had turned away from them to wash her hands in the large farmhouse sink. "It's them!"

Aunt Dotty had grabbed a towel and rotated to face them, a smile stretching across a familiar face. She looked like a combination of Viera and her father. "I believe you are correct. It certainly is them. My niece, who looks a lot like me and Lloyd, and her stunningly beautiful girlfriend, who I hope she can figure out how to keep."

Viera could feel all the warring emotions from the people in the room. Aunt Dotty's amusement and concern. Amanda's shock and excitement. Mother's fear and hope, and Father's hope that everything would turn out. She had to work to not tremble at everyone's heightened emotions.

She heard her breathing get choppy as she smiled at Aunt Dotty and Amanda. Before she could respond, Thorn slipped an arm around her waist, giving her a squeeze. "I'm more worried about her slipping away from me. She's quite the catch, don't you know."

Between the touch and what Thorn said, some of the tension released, and Viera's shoulders relaxed. She focused on Amanda. "So, you're the only one in this room who actually watches the news … good to know."

Aunt Dotty cackled. "News? No. That's me. She's on social media. She's seen the memes. They're great, by the way. Have you seen any of them?"

Viera couldn't stop the groan and probably only stayed standing because of Thorn. "No, I've avoided them. Are they horrible?"

The knocking of glass on granite got them all looking over at Father. "Memes? Social media? News? What is this all about?"

Amanda found her voice again. "But … it's you two! Here in this house." She started to bounce like she'd been given a gift. "Like, I can touch you." Her eyes widened. "I could get a picture with you two and post it and become like … Insta-famous or something."

After rubbing her temples, Viera searched first Amanda's face, hopeful and a bit manic, then her aunt's amused but not worried expression, and finally Thorn's. "Can we get someone to zap all the memes? Make them all go away? Maybe one of the qynads or a dwarf? Do we know any tech-wizards?"

"Probably not. They're like roaches. Once they're out there, that's it. Out for life. But if we could, wouldn't you want to see them first? Aren't you even a bit curious?"

"No. And, God, I'm suddenly even more thrilled about tomorrow. Like, you can't even believe how excited."

"Why?" Mother handed each of them a mimosa. "What's happening tomorrow?"

Amanda's mouth dropped open. "Is that when you're leaving?"

Aunt Dotty slapped the back of her head. "How about you stop now. You know how I started off playing dumb? Now it's time for you to play smart, my brilliant wife."

There was a moment of silence in the kitchen, then Amanda's hands flew up to cover her face. "Oh, my God, I'm so sorry. I don't know what came over me. Dots, you're right, I need to stop and let these two explain everything themselves." Her hands fell to her side. "But afterward, maybe we can talk?"

With a sigh, Viera nodded. "Yeah, maybe later."

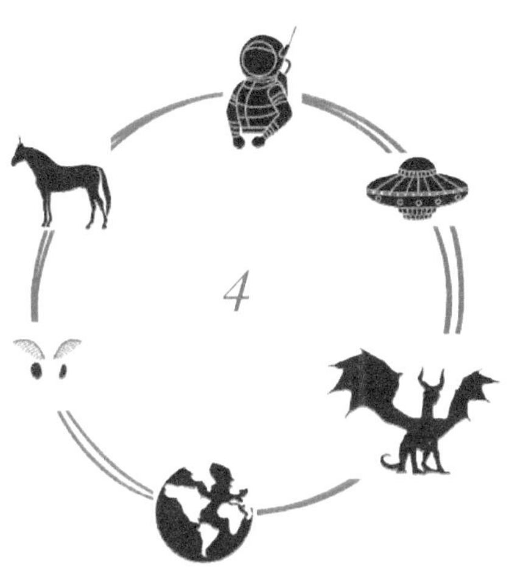

You Want What Now?

Betsy

As soon as Betsy stepped off the elevator, Miranda smiled warmly, her short brunette hair perfectly styled, as always, and handed her a coffee and a bag. "I know you were here yesterday, and I saw you were on schedule for today as well. There's a nice, locally owned coffee shop down the street from my condo. I thought I'd bring you their Friday special."

Sniffing the cup, Betsy smelled cinnamon. "Is this a cinnamon café?"

"It's a cinnamon bun mocha with their world-famous monkey bread. It's so good that people from all over the city come to get it." Miranda's brown eyes twinkled with mirth. "I know the owners, so I have a standing order."

One of Betsy's eyebrows rose. "Am I stealing your breakfast?"

"No." She smirked. "I stopped in last night on my way home. I told them I'd need a double order."

"Thank you." Betsy could hear the need for the treat in her own voice. *I hope Orson knows the treasure he has in that woman!*

Taking the bag, she opened the conference room door and paused when she saw Juk. Of all the people she didn't want to see, he was near the top of the list. Thinking about it, she shouldn't have been surprised he was there. "Morning, Juk. Happy Friday." Years of practice meant she was sure he couldn't hear the disdain she felt. He'd have to do a lot to win back any respect.

At least he hadn't been part of yesterday's ordeal. He's so young. If Orson wants me to train him, he'll be old and gray before he's up to snuff.

"Betsy!" Juk started to stand but stopped at Betsy's raised eyebrow. She chose a seat across and one over from him. Though the table could seat sixteen, they usually occupied the center chairs. She pulled out her monkey bread as he spoke. "I'm sorry I missed all the fun yesterday. Mr. Mard told me I wouldn't be needed. I tried to tell him we work well together, and you'd want me there, but alas, he thought otherwise." His smile could've been plastered in a magazine.

Betsy sipped her coffee. It was amazing. She tore off a piece of the bread, and the warm, gooey treat soothed the annoyance at sharing space with only Juk. "Well, you did tell me on the phone that you have several other people you work with. I know I'm only one person on your *massive list* and you can't always clear your calendar for me."

It still irked her that when she had called him for an immediate meeting, he'd tried to put her off for a week. When he'd been assigned as her point person, he'd claimed to have read all the files, but the arrogance of ignoring her proved he hadn't.

The biggest thing her contacts had to know was that if she called, it was a priority. She'd read the files herself, even though they were top secret and, technically, she wasn't an agent. There wasn't anything she didn't have clearance for. She and her dad had created this department years ago. Betsy knew her demands were always considered a top priority by everyone in this department, but all the top brass knew that what she needed, she should get. For some reason, it didn't travel down to the new people.

Juk's mouth tightened. "Right, I meant to apologize for that. I don't know what I was thinking ... not immediately hearing your words. You won't need to go to Mr. Mard again."

Before anything else could be said, the door opened, and the man himself walked in. "Oh, good, you're both here." He placed a box on the table. "I brought some muffins ... I don't want anyone to leave hungry."

The monkey bread was almost gone. The serving hadn't been large, but it had been sweet, a nice compliment to the dark coffee. She gazed at the muffins ... *maybe in a few minutes.* "Okay, Orson, I was here yesterday and I'm here today, but

I don't want to spend my weekend in New York. It's been a hell of a week, and I'm ready to be back home and have some down time. Why did you want me to return?"

Orson's smile was warm and welcoming. Everything Juk's wasn't. The boy had a lot to learn. "I just want the three of us to be on the same page moving forward. I want a plan in place so we're ready to face the fallout of the krottel invasion and that fire display at yesterday's press conference."

Juk's eyes narrowed, and he opened the folder in front of him, paging through a stack of papers. "I'm sorry, sir. I've been offline for the last twenty-four hours. I knew you'd be at the conference, so I shut my door to catch up with some of my other responsibilities. I was here late last night, and when I got in this morning, I came right here. I figured I'd get an email if there were any emergencies."

With a clenched jaw, Betsy stared blankly at Juk. *Of course he had. He has one job.* One of her brows rose slowly as Orson sighed. "Mr. Hopkins, Juk, when you attend one of these meetings, especially with Pillar Doeth, I expect you to be on top of everything. I want you to know more than anyone in the room." He removed his glasses and placed them on the table, then rubbed his face. "You know what I'm doing is really your job. I want to work from home. I'm tired of being in the city. Can I trust you to be the point person?"

It was only years of this life that kept Betsy's face neutral. She'd known Orson since he started as a young buck. Now in his sixties, his rise in the department was based on brilliance and nothing else. Betsy was ready to place bets on whether Juk would last more than a handful of years.

You could read a novel off the range of emotions that crossed Juk's face. His forehead scrunched, his eyes squinted, and his lip popped up on the left side. Then, as he gazed toward the ceiling, his mouth pursed tight. Finally, his face cleared, and he leaned back, arms crossed. "I knew everything the four of you were going to talk about and had a lot of back work that I figured, with everything that's about to happen, I wouldn't have time to do. Sir, you were there, so I made an executive decision."

Orson had a tell. His right eye twitched ... once, maybe twice when he was really angry. You had to watch to see it. Most didn't know this about him, but Betsy saw the double twitch. "The recorded part, where we were on stage, wasn't very long. Being my main representative to the Pillars, I expect you to watch *every* press conference that Pillar Doeth or any other Pillar is part of. Or if the aliens happen to be part of a live telecast, I expect you to drop whatever you're doing and pay attention. Is that a clear enough directive, Mr. Hopkins?"

Historically, hiring people for this department took a long time. Quite a few employees were children of former employees, with their parents or grandparents as references. It often led to overly arrogant agents. Moreover, working with the Pillars and aliens meant a longer and deeper background check. Most new employees figured that out fast and knew that getting fired wasn't likely ... it wasn't impossible, but it also didn't happen often. Most eventually learned.

But why do I end up with the worst of them?

"Yes, sir." Juk had sat up straighter during the talk down. "I understand. Did I miss anything?"

Betsy held her hand up to him, palm up. "Wait." She turned to Orson. "How many press conferences do you anticipate Pillar involvement in?"

Her friend smiled, the tension in the room dropping. He leaned forward to grab a chocolate muffin. "Well, that's just it. As I see it, all of them. You lot are the experts." Dread grasped Betsy, and she sipped her coffee, trying to conceal any reaction. After years of hiding, even the youngest of the Pillars wouldn't want their faces splashed to the public. He continued. "The chanzii are leaving. The first question on my mind is, do you know if we'll have any alien representatives working with us? It would be nice to have help as we see an influx of other aliens, as I'm sure we will, and more importantly, help educate our people." He leaned back. "With Commander Firoza heading back to Abritos, it would be nice if we could find someone."

"I don't know. She and Viera leave tomorrow, and I'll be seeing them off. If you'd like, I can ask. Commander Firoza may have an idea." Betsy sipped her coffee. "But you're changing the subject."

"Not really." He leaned back. "Something huge just happened. I think you know that. Not only has the entire world just learned about aliens, but they've learned that there are many races out there, some that we, the government, have known about for years. Moreover, we work with them in peace." He sighed. "On top of that, they learned that there is magic in the universe. To some, their science fiction and fantasy dreams came true in one fell swoop." He winked. "Can you imagine if they knew who your—"

"Don't. That is on a need-to-know basis, and *no one* needs to know that."

Juk's brow knit. "Wait, who are we talking about?" He started leafing through the papers again.

"You won't find it in there, son. Pillar Doeth cleared all mentions from the database and set a virus so that if it were mentioned, our whole system would crash. She can be diabolical. Don't get on her bad side if you can help it." He sounded amused.

In one of the only smart actions she'd seen from the boy since meeting him, he blanched.

Betsy sighed. "So, what you're hinting at is you want the Pillars to hold regular press conferences to help inform the masses. You want us to disseminate the real information over and over in the hopes that something sticks."

Orson beamed. "I knew you'd get it. Now, you have Juk to work with in the New York office. I know you'll be working from Wisconsin, but I'd like you to hold an in-person conference each Thursday. Juk will set them up all over the world. We can get interpreters. This way, everyone can ask questions if they have them. We'll get a website set up so questions can be sent in, and we'll assemble a crew to answer them. We can have a public page where the most common questions are answered by you or any of the other Pillars, or we can set up a panel here to submit answers."

"Let me speak with the others tonight and get back to you. I'll send Juk an update by noon tomorrow, so your engineers have time to get this set up by Monday." Betsy decided the blueberry muffins looked good and took one. "Do you know where Thursday's conference will be?"

Both Orson and Betsy looked at Juk, who shrank in his seat. Smiling wide, like the cat who'd cornered a mouse, Betsy almost purred, "This is why you never come to one of these meetings unprepared. Take this as the learning opportunity it is, or you won't be invited next time."

He slowly nodded. "Right." His pen flew over a notepad. "Thursday's press conference, don't piss off the Pillars." His gaze popped up to Betsy's.

"Can you really code well enough to create a virus, or did you have a hacker friend help you?"

She debated using magic to slap him silly. Orson merely groaned, shaking his head. "That question is right up there with you asking me if I know how to send an email, boy wonder. You have two choices: guess at the answer or test and find out."

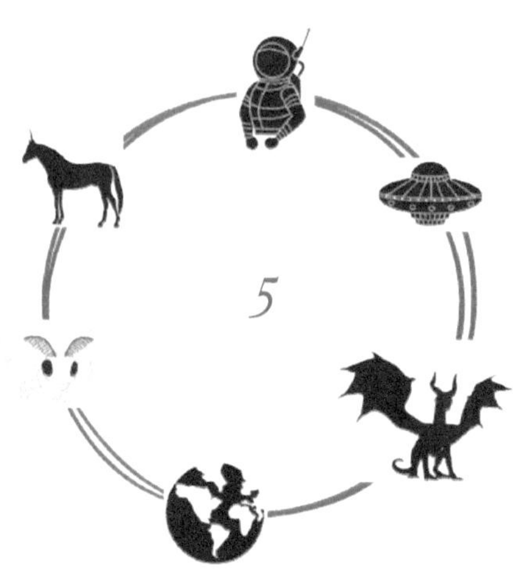

I'm Not the Boss of You

Betsy

Betsy swam after transporting from New York to home. She'd forgotten she'd made her pool salt water after Viera discovered that her second-grade student Tiffany was a cambpulpo shifter. Her parents had decided to vacation on Earth roughly sixteen years ago but never checked in. When their daughter had been found alone and sent into foster care and then adopted, they never even considered contacting any of the Pillars.

The whole situation still made Betsy burn with anger. The parents hid in the ocean in their octopus form, letting Tiffany grow up with humans who had no idea who she was or why she aged so slowly. It was only Viera's ability to read memories that had allowed her to find the girl hiding in her class. *So much time and suffering could've been avoided if they'd just followed protocol.*

She had a meeting with the other Pillars to prepare for and didn't have time to worry about the type of water in her pool. She needed to get ready.

After her shower, Betsy dressed in a comfortable tank top and shorts. The two ven she'd adopted flew around her, excited she'd finally arrived home. Buttercup and Wes were a delight to her, and she tried to give them each scritches and enough time to learn the boundaries of her property before exploring outdoors. Until then, they were confined to her house. She knew they wanted to stretch their wings and put it on her short list of priorities.

The oversized moth-looking creatures would scare anyone who didn't know what they were, but once the general population learned about them ... She couldn't imagine the frenzy these cute beasties would cause on Earth.

Maybe I should bring them to my press conferences. They'd win more people over than just about any other alien. Once people learn the "unicorns" are assholes, all bets are off.

She knew she had to get logged on soon, but first, she wanted to eat a real meal. With all the different time zones, getting a convenient meal ... wasn't.

Instead of heading to her office downtown, Betsy went to her home office. She'd sent out a scheduled meeting for three in the afternoon her time, or fifteen hundred hours. The most inconvenient times would be for Zuza in London, who was six hours ahead, and Ania in Sydney at thirteen hours ahead. It would be tomorrow for her and early morning.

All the Pillars would take calls at all hours. They knew that when something important came up, sleep could be made up later.

Betsy logged onto the computer and waited for the boxes to fill with the faces of the other people she'd thought were the only magic holders on Earth ... until Viera ... until this town.

Marco popped in first with his sparkling brown eyes and short black hair. He always looked full of youthful zeal. "Hiya, Betsy, nice job yesterday. You only looked slightly annoyed at that interruption. Can't wait to hear *that* story."

As he spoke, Ania, the oldest of them, logged on. With orangish-red curly hair and green eyes, she made a face hearing the end of Marco's comment. "I should've retired and left the planet ten years ago."

The other two came online as she spoke. Zuza shook his head, crystalline blue eyes sparkling. "Oh, no. Not allowed. You are a fixture here on Earth, and now you're needed more than ever. If you leave, we'll only have four Pillars. One of us has to start procreating!"

Kafi leaned in, his boyish face the most serious-looking of them all. "Betsy, was that display real? Are there more magic users around?" He was obviously ignoring Zuza's comment.

Betsy sipped her tea. "It seems so, but that mystery still needs to be unraveled. There were three of them who claimed to be able to imbue items, but their ages weren't affected." She went on to explain the basics of the meeting the day before.

Ania sneered. "What the hell? A whole town of people who can imbue? The freaking unicorn is going to have a hay day!"

Marco laughed. "Isn't 'unicorn' a modern word? When did you stop using 'yonat?'"

"When Flower Prancer continued to annoy me more and more. He's such a horse's ass," she said, waggling her brows as everyone else smiled or laughed. "But more than them, the dwarves need to know. They've always been the only ones who consistently had wizards and Elders who could imbue. What will they think of this group of magic wielders?" She shook her head. "When do we let word out about this town?"

"Not right away." Betsy shook her head. "I need to figure out more about them. There's something strange about the people I met. I don't think they had cell phones on them, or any watches. They were the strangest group. I don't know why, but they triggered my warning bells."

Zuza spun in his chair. "You said they were normal human ages?" He gazed at the large bookcase behind him. His finger traced along row after row of books, tapping here and there until he finally selected one.

"Yeah, why? Do you have an idea?"

He faced his camera again. "I do." A wry smile crossed his face. "I remember getting this book from my dad years ago. He'd gotten it from someone on Torville Three? Maybe?"

"Three?" Kafi shook his head. "There is no Torville Station Number Three."

"There was several centuries ago." A far-off look took over Ania's face. "When I was a girl, maybe Marco's age ... maybe even younger. In my thirties or forties? My family went there as my first adventure into space. It was my one-year adventure in space to learn Galactic Standard and learn about aliens. It was one of the better spots at the time." She shook her head. "Anyway, several years later, not many, ten, twenty maybe, the kucing and anjing went to war, and that station got destroyed in the crossfire."

Kafi squinted. "No, wait, I have this. Those beings are rare and usually stay on-planet, but isn't that a catlike race and a doglike race? Like, literally cats versus dogs?"

Everyone chuckled at his indignation.

Zuza said, "Don't let *them* hear you say that. Not if you want to survive. They know about Earth, and that joke doesn't translate well. Got it?" He raised an eyebrow. "Okay, it's like I remembered. There is a weird subset of magic users, very rare, who don't use magic from within themselves but from the world around them. Because of the field's energy, it disrupts other fields around them, including electronics. There was a group who used magic this way on a planet. A group transported down and all their electronics shorted out. It took time to figure out what was happening."

"Okay, so we have a working theory on this town." Ania chuckled. "Of imbuers? Gods above, this is going to cause intergalactic heads to explode. At least it isn't innate. They can't be very strong, or we'd have a whole new invasion."

"That isn't all," Betsy continued. She went on to talk about her early meeting with Orson and Juk. Everyone fell silent, and despite being on the computer screen, she could feel everyone watching her. "What? I'm not the leader of this group or the spokesperson. It doesn't have to be me. Any one of us can represent the Pillars at these press conferences."

Marco, with a twinkle in his eyes, said, "Who got on stage yesterday?"

Ania laughed in a manner that said the matter was shut.

For fuck's sake. We've all been working together for way too long!

"How about this," Marco said, sounding a bit contrite. "While you're globe-trotting, spreading our secrets around the world in a manner we've all dreaded, and being amazing on camera, I'll start searching the web for conspiracy groups that pop up. You know this is going to bring out the crazies."

Kafi nodded. "I'll take on the religious angle and social circles. Someone is bound to try to come after us. You know, Betsy, in the end, only giving them one of our names and faces really is for the best."

She groaned, hating that he was right.

"I can take on the academics." Zuza volunteered. "I'd like to say they're more learned and ready to be levelheaded, but we all know they'll find a way to take this to the extreme as well."

"I'll search for other magical towns." Ania looked much more serious. "If you're going to be our face, the rest of us need to be the eyes, ears, and research behind what you're doing. You'll stir the possum in the next few weeks ... we'll be your minions."

The migraine pounded in Betsy's head.

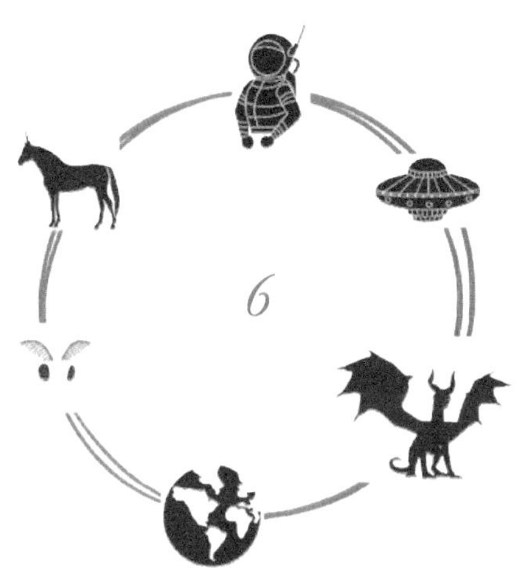

Home Sweet Home

Pearl

"I am so ready to be out of this car." Cassidy shut her book loudly and tossed it onto the seat next to her.

Watching the road signs, Pearl lifted the lever and pushed her seat back so she could see her friend better. "We're like five minutes from Oz. I think you can make it."

Devlin sighed. "I still can't believe the last few days. The government knows who we are. Those Pillar people have our names. They knew our last names which means they can find us. Our secrecy, our privacy, our security ... it's all gone."

With a pull on the lever, Pearl sat back up. "It'll be fine. Just breathe. Our town has stayed hidden because it was safer in a world that didn't believe. With aliens, an invasion, and the Pillars, what Cassidy did is such a non-issue. Don't worry. And even if people talk about the general masses having magic, no one else will figure out it was us."

"Pearl, you're brilliant but naive. If the government can find us, so can the conspiracy nuts. You do understand our life as a private community is over."

"I think you're wrong." The certainty that filled her gut couldn't be denied. She just knew that what her friend had done was nothing compared to everything else. "Devlin, there were freaking dragons flying around the skies of Chicago breathing fire. I really think there are more sensational things than us."

He sighed dramatically. "You're forgetting, just because we don't spend our life on the internet doesn't mean most of the world doesn't. There will be people who will focus on that person in the crowd who made the presenters look like fools. Even if it isn't the immediate top story, it will eventually be the focus of social media. Give it time."

Cassidy hummed in the back, a smirk on her face. "I'm going to be famous."

Pearl scoffed. "No, you won't, that's the point. There's a better-than-good chance none of the cameras were on us. The only people who know who we are were in that room, and they have to deal with everyone else in the world. If we are on their to-do list, we won't be very high."

With a grunt that probably reiterated her naïveté, Devlin continued to navigate the last few blocks through town to drop them off.

He dropped Cassidy off first before taking Pearl home.

She thought about the last few days. The three of them had heard about the press conference and had wanted to know what the official word about the aliens would be. Her mom, the mayor, hadn't wanted Pearl and Cassidy to travel alone, and though old enough to make their own choices, they'd agreed to ask Devlin. Not only was he nice and powerful, but he paid more attention to the outside world than most of Oz.

Pearl had been surprised by how honest it had all been. She knew governments were all about covering things up. Moreover, she hadn't expected to meet the presenters personally. If only Cassidy had controlled herself.

When they got to her house, Devlin followed her in. "Mom, Dad, I'm home! And Devlin's with me," she yelled, heading to the living room and flopping down on a recliner.

Devlin veered into the kitchen. "Do you want something to drink? Soda?"

"Yeah, that'll work."

Her parents came up from the basement and hugged her before sitting on the couch. "Welcome back," Mom said. "How was the trip?"

After handing her a drink, Devlin sat in the other recliner. "It was much more eventful than any of us could've planned or hoped for."

Mom's face stiffened and she morphed into the mayor. "Eventful?"

He sighed. "Yeah. Apparently, there are five Pillars living on Earth who can do a lot of pretty sophisticated magic. I don't know the extent of it, but it's more than we do in town. They've been doing their thing as well as working with a select representation of aliens for ... God, I don't know, centuries. It wasn't really clear how long."

While Mom continued to hold herself tight, Dad looked contemplative.

"That doesn't sound too bad. From what we saw, that's what we figured. That fight in Chicago obviously had aliens, and we saw some sort of magic being used. It didn't look like anything we do, save the fire. Except for—" Dad's words were interrupted by Dulaine, Pearl's eleven-year-old sister running in from the back hall to give Pearl a tackle hug. "You know," Dad continued, not naming Dulaine personally, "just about everyone can do fire magic. It's the first real sign a person can use magic."

With her wide gray eyes, Dulaine gazed up at Pearl. "I can't make fire. Does that mean I'm not a witch? Am I broken?"

Pearl hugged her sister in a tight squeeze. "There is nothing wrong with you, Du-Drop. You are perfect, just the way you are."

This was a conversation they'd had several times since Pearl had returned from college. No one would make her sister feel less than she was.

Despite Pearl's conviction, the adults in the room eyed each other, worry etched on their faces. By eleven, Dulaine should be showing some affinity toward magic. If she didn't soon, she'd be the first person in the town of Oz to be without magic in several generations. There were people from other locations who married in and weren't magical, but the kids always bred true.

Both Mom and Dad were from town and had magic. The fact that Dulaine could be without it worried everyone. But Pearl knew, deep down, that her sister wasn't a magical dud.

Pearl sighed, still a bit annoyed at her friend's spontaneity but knowing it was that free spirit she loved so much. "Cassidy did some magic. The people on stage found out about us."

Mom practically leapt from her seat. Before she could say anything, Devlin's hands shot out to stop her. "Wait, Vicky, listen. I know this sounds bad, but it isn't. We spent the last two days in the car talking about it. These people know about magic. It isn't like they're freaking out about us. Moreover, when they spoke to us privately—"

"They what now?" Mom's voice was low ... dangerous.

"Mom. Listen. They pulled us into a conference room so the general media wouldn't be able to overhear us. We may have gotten more from them than they got from us. The person running the meeting, this woman named Betsy, God, Mom, she looked like she was Devlin's age, but to hear the group talk, she was ancient, like *old* old."

Mom's eyes were closed, and she looked pained. Dad rubbed his face but, as always, let Mom take point.

Devlin shook his head. "I know she said she was ten times my age, but there's no way."

Mom's eyes popped open. "Wait ... Pillar? Old? Shit. I think I know who and what you're talking about. I have a journal. Porter, go get that book on the shelf by my side of the bed. Leather bound, old."

He shrugged and ambled off. They waited, and a few minutes later, Dad returned with what Mom wanted. She looked off for a moment, then said,

"This was something my ... I don't know, great-great-great-grandma kept, maybe. Maybe more?" She flipped through the journal, reading a page here and there. "Okay, this is it."

"I met a woman today walking with a gray horse. Of all the insane things, I thought I saw her talking to the horse. Now, I've seen people speak to animals, but in my need to gather ingredients in the field, I'd used a see-me-not spell. I was also behind a big rock. She asked the animal, 'Do I have to work with him? He's so arrogant.'

The gray horse, believe it or not, stamped his foot and swished his tail, then the beast said, 'Yes, Betsy, Flower Prancer is newly risen and will get mellower with age.'

'Fine, Star Dancer, because of the respect I have for you, I will do this.'

'Pillar Doeth, you bring your family honor. I give you this pendant as a thank you.'"

Mom looked up at the people in the room. "You don't think this is the same Betsy, do you? This was two hundred years ago ... maybe less."

Pearl felt the blood drain from her face. She'd met someone centuries old and the stories she'd told appeared to be real.

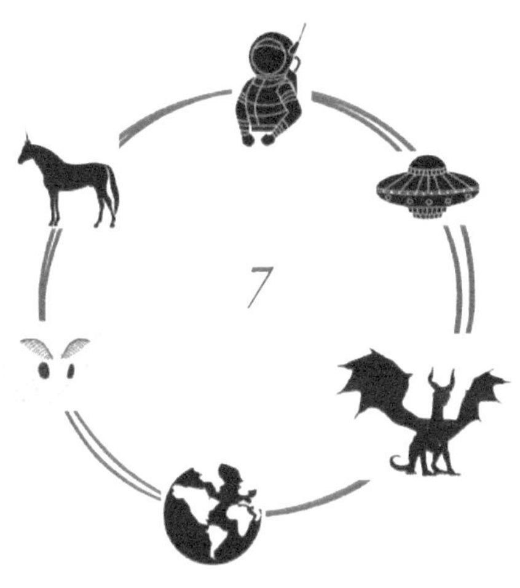

7

A Sweet Surprise

Betsy

Betsy sat in Thorn's kitchen, drinking coffee and eating a breakfast sandwich. Thorn and Viera sat with her. Scout, Thorn's son, had already taken the ven to the athletic center with the luggage. Horax, one of Thorn's main personnel and an enormous blue qynad, small for his kind but still a huge dragon by human standards, and

Juniper, an ensign but a friend of the family who often watched Scout, were there organizing those who were heading off-world.

With the Elders' decision, the krottel evacuated Abritos, allowing Thorn's people, the chanzii, to finally go home. Before they all could leave, a smaller group, including Thorn and Viera, would be heading to the planet to ensure it was ready for habitation. A full plan for leaving Earth had been presented to both the Pillars and the government.

Because aliens were now known to the general population, Orson and Betsy decided to allow more chanzii to leave in each phase, though not by much in this first wave. They figured the empty houses could now be explained. Thorn was reviewing the last details of who was going and who was staying and updating the lists on the master database Betsy and the government kept.

Betsy sipped her coffee. "Okay, so your aunt's wife—"

"Amanda," Viera said, amusement evident on her face.

"Okay, Amanda, she fangirled on both of you?"

Thorn looked up from her tablet, chuckling. "It was cute. Before we could get to her starry-eyed adoration, we had to backtrack to the parents."

"Who knew nothing," Viera said with finality. "You know them. They hide from knowing anything about anything. I was surprised they knew about the invasion at all."

Both Betsy's eyebrows shot up. "Really? It'd been less than a week. How did they know that much?"

Viera scoffed. "They'd gone 'to play golf' with some friends at their club."

"I still don't know why you air quote that." Thorn gazed at Viera, looking confused.

With a snort, Viera sipped her coffee. "Because Dad sits at the bar with his friends watching the latest game—football, baseball, tennis, doesn't matter—and Mom sits by the pool drinking margaritas with her friends. The club offers golf, but I doubt they've played once." Her smile widened. "It's too hot and humid." They both laughed. "Anyway, the TV wasn't showing any games after Dad ordered his beer. He had a front-row ticket to see all of it. You'd think after that, he'd pay attention to some of the fall out, but as he said, anything worth knowing, someone would tell him about later."

Betsy debated exasperation versus amusement. She'd heard a lot about Viera's parents for years, but this confirmed a lot. "An alien invasion didn't convince them to watch any follow-up news? Or maybe call you since you live so close?"

"Well, that's just it. Mom *did* call me on Thursday. She asked if I was okay. That's when we discussed Thorn and I coming out to have dinner. Then, with everything happening so fast ... well, yeah."

The conversation went silent for a moment. Betsy thought about the number of changes the world had undergone, from the krottel invasion Monday to her best friend leaving later today. "You told them you were leaving?"

A sad smile slowly formed on Viera's face. "Yeah. Once we got through all the questions. I had to explain aliens and magic to everyone. Then Thorn shifted. I thought Mom would faint from information overload and Amanda would faint from stimulation overload." Thorn snorted at her description. "We finally ate, and everyone calmed down. Mom worried she'd never see me again, but we assured her I'd be back. I explained I'd be sending data packages a few times a year and would include letters to them. I told them they could email you if they wanted to respond. I gave them your email ... I hope that's okay."

"Until they spam me, and I have to wipe their memories," Betsy said with a blank expression.

Viera leaned over and hugged her. "Thank you." She bit her lower lip. "I may take you up on that memory wipe, I hope you know."

Betsy chuckled. This was why they were friends.

Once they were done eating, they cleaned up their dishes. Thorn gazed around the house. "You know, I'm really happy about heading home, but I'm also going to miss this place."

Betsy nodded. "What's going to happen with the empty houses? Did you submit your plan? I've been running around ... too much to check."

"Violet will handle the final cleanup. As homes are vacated, cleaned, and ready for resale, she'll handle finding the right people to work through the logistics in each area. We'll send ten percent of all profits to the government, five to the Pillars, and the rest will go to the families to help with relocation expenses. Torville Station Number Six did a bit of Earth exchange before. I'm guessing they will jump at the opportunity to work with Earth money again, especially if the boarder is opening up in the foreseeable future."

"Torville will take a big percentage of the profits, with fifteen percent going to the Pillars and government. Are your people okay with that?"

Thorn shrugged. "It'll still be plenty of money."

"And Violet is taking over? You're not working with our people? I take it you met Juk, and he didn't impress you?" Betsy grimaced. "Too bad we had to get a new point person at this stage of the game."

"I'd rather keep everything in-house anyway, and Violet volunteered to stay around and act as our liaison."

A small thrill worked its way up Betsy's spine at the thought of working with Violet. She didn't know the chanziian major well, and she lived on the West Coast, but the few times they'd interacted had been memorable.

The three headed toward the athletic center, where everyone departing for Abritos planned to meet. When they got there, the main room teemed with beings.

The number of people milling about the space—there had to be several hundred—amazed Betsy. *They make the large room appear tiny.* "This many people are leaving?"

"No, Pillar Doeth, some are here to say goodbye to friends." Horax lumbered over to them, amazingly agile for such a large creature. The qynad's blue scales, so like a dragon from Earth fantasy, shone in the sun that slanted in from the high windows.

Glancing up, Betsy saw Beaver, her baby ven's mother, flying with the remaining three babies. They were zooming in circles above the crowd, staying out of the way. *I hope Thorn enjoys her son's pets. I know Viera does.*

"Horax!" Betsy practically yelled to be heard over the din of all the people in the room. She gave the large beast a hug. "Are you staying? I could use help during all the press conferences I have to give."

"No." Thorn's voice was that of the commander of the chanzii people. There was no room for discussion. "He is an integral part of my crew. It'd be like asking for Juniper, which is also a hard 'no,' if you're wondering."

"You know ..." Betsy let one eyebrow rise slowly. "Now that aliens are known to the general population, you're taking all my allies away." Then she laughed at Thorn's hard stare.

"You are right, Pillar Doeth. I shall be leaving with them. Ms. Kor's magic is not trained." Flower Prancer, the cantankerous yonat himself, cut through the throngs of people to approach them. His arrogant speech was easy to hear despite the noise of the room. "She is a danger without a caretaker."

If he did stay, the people of Earth would learn that unicorns were assholes, and this one looks like every child's dream, white with a rainbow mane and tail. He's the one alien I'll be happy to see leave.

Despite her thoughts, Betsy made sure to keep tight control over her features. Out of the corner of her eye, she saw Viera tense. Thorn slid an arm around her friend's waist. Despite Viera's anger, Betsy wasn't sure who she felt worse for. She knew Viera could hold her own, and once she mastered her three proficiencies, she'd be downright unstoppable.

Thorn's eyes narrowed dangerously as she looked at the yonat.

Before she could say anything to him, Xantay, a large red qynad, approached. Betsy hadn't seen her in several years ... decades? "Commander Firoza, Pillar Doeth." Her voice was low and gravely, though not unpleasant. The black markings on the ends of her wings shimmered in the sun's light.

After a moment to recompose, Thorn smiled, turning to the newcomer. "Yes, Xantay. How can I help you? I didn't know you were on Earth."

"I've been asked to act as liaison to Earth for the qynads now that the humans know about us." A low grumble came from her chest, signaling her pleasure for the assignment.

"Being the first must be an honor. I'm honored to welcome you to Earth, young one." Betsy nodded to Xantay, amused at Earth's new ally.

Thorn smiled wide. "I'm glad. Your council couldn't have selected a better representative. I'll let Major North know you'll be around. I know you'll be officially checking in with the Pillars, but please include her as well."

"Of course. Are there any other liaisons on-planet?"

Everyone looked at Betsy. She shrugged. "Not that I know of … well, beyond Toby … the Fing, but he won't be coming to any meetings."

Flower Prancer's tail swished. "We need to get going. If we hear anything on Torville Station Number Six, we'll be sure to send a message back to either you or Major North." His head swung to Thorn. "Commander Firoza, when did Major Violet North get the promotion? I hadn't heard anything about that?"

Though Betsy hadn't either, she didn't assume that a non-chanziian would.

Thorn's smile grew nasty. "Well, that would be internal to the chanziian people, Flower Prancer, and not the Elders. If you don't mind, I have a couple more things to tell Pillar Doeth." She glanced around. "And it seems Horax has already transported up to the ship. He and Juniper are in charge of getting everyone else up in an orderly manner. I'll be up soon."

She turned her back and slid an arm around Betsy's, leading her toward Violet, who had entered the building. When the chanzii came to Earth, they'd needed regional leaders to give their people someone to go to if they needed help, had questions, or got into trouble. Violet headed the Western United States.

Seeing the other chanzii warmed Betsy in a way she wasn't ready to admit. Thorn reached out a hand. "Violet."

"Commander."

"I am promoting you, effective immediately, to major. Since you're staying here to do ... well, everything, you'll need the authority." Thorn winked. "Congratulations. I'm sorry I couldn't do more to celebrate."

Violet's eyes widened and her mouth dropped open. Then she closed it and opened it again as if trying to figure out what to say.

"I could take you out for a celebration," Betsy said, amused by her reaction. *Why did I do that?*

Violet's eyes widened more, and she blushed. "I'd like that."

Thorn smiled wide. "Perfect. Since the two of you will be working together a lot over the next few weeks, this is a great time to iron things out. Now, I need to head out. The yonat, though arrogant, wasn't wrong."

Thorn hugged each of them. Then Viera ran over to do the same. Slowly, the room emptied of everyone heading back to Abritos.

Standing next to the chanziian major, Betsy was both sad to see her friends go and excited about working with Violet.

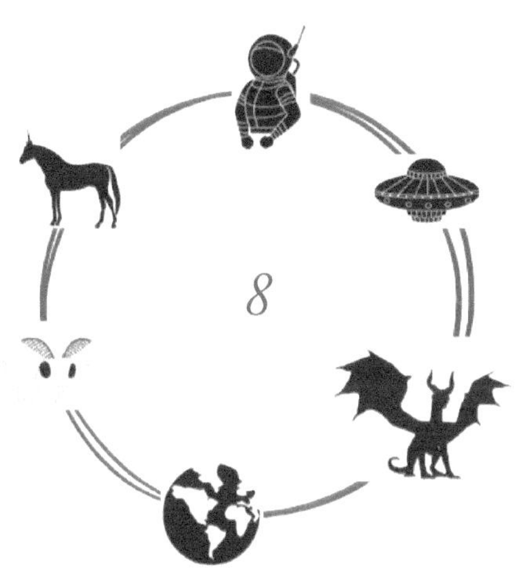

Welcome to Wisconsin

Betsy

Once the athletic center was empty of everyone leaving for Torville Station Number Six, Betsy relaxed. Step one was complete. Most of the chanzii headed out now that their friends were gone.

When there were only three of them left, Betsy turned to Xantay. "So, now that you're on Earth, tell me, how did one so young get the position of liaison of Earth?"

The red qynad began to bounce, her excitement filling the room. "Oh, my gods, you wouldn't believe it, I was on the Ziner with Dad, I mean Horax, I mean—"

"Xantay, breathe," Betsy interrupted. "We're not in a hurry. You don't have to get all the words out in under a minute."

A rumble of amusement vibrated out of the large red creature. Violet laughed as well. They both knew Horax's daughter and how much she loved to talk. "Sorry. Well, anyway, I was available and right here. We got a communiqué from the planet, I mean Grarrou, that they may send someone else, but if I show that I'm doing a good job ... and both you and the best liaison *ever*," she shot a look over to Violet, "tell them I'm doing a good job, I may be able to keep my position. I'm of age. I've held my position on the Ziner for five years, even before the krottel, and before that, I was doing similar work back home."

Betsy nodded throughout her speech. "Okay, that all sounds good. And until I find a place for you to stay, or rather, the government does, where are you hoping to live?"

"Well, Dad ... Horax, stayed on the *Ziner*, which, of course, just left. They did leave me a shuttle, but though it's big enough for me, it's cramped. I thought I'd spend most of my time on the island the government gave the chanzii for alien shore leave during my downtime and be wherever you need me otherwise."

Betsy briefly considered her plot of land. It was large with a wooded area that would work, but the island had privacy and good communication. "That sounds perfect. Why don't you get yourself situated. I assume you're not completely alone? Do you have a crew?"

"I do. I have two crew members, a kucing named Inxoka and another qynad named Tarako. I believe we can all coexist well on the island."

"If you don't mind, maybe I or"—Betsy shot a quick look at Violet—"maybe we can come and visit on Monday or Tuesday. That way, we can see how things are going. Make sure you don't need anything."

Xantay rumbled low in her chest in pleasure. The sound resembled rocks rubbing together, though it was akin to a cat's purr. "Sounds great, Pillar Doeth. I will see you then." She turned to Violet. "*Major* North. Congratulations on your promotion."

Violet smiled, watching the youthful qynad practically skip across the room. When she got toward the center, she transported away, leaving the two alone. Violet shifted her gaze to Betsy. "You don't have to take me out to dinner, you know."

"Of course I do ... unless you were planning to head back to the West Coast."

The other woman blushed. "Oh, no. Actually, I was thinking of relocating here. With Thorn leaving, I thought it would be easier to be closer to you for any meetings we may have." Her face reddened more. "Transporting is easy—I had to do it to get to work when I was on Abritos—but I really appreciate the simpler transport you have here on Earth."

One of Betsy's brows rose. "You like to drive?"

"I do. But I also love your bikes. They're so easy to get around on, and the breeze is amazing."

"You do know we have snow half the year here."

Violet laughed. "Yes, but less rain, so the trade-off seems worth it."

"Okay. Have you already found a house? Are you moving into one of the ones here?" Betsy waved vaguely around the athletic center but meant Soaring Arbor Heights, the chanzii subdivision.

"I spoke with Thorn, and I thought I'd just take over her place. There's no way she's coming back, not full-time. When she does return, if I take over her home, she'll have a place she's used to for a home base. I figure I can keep Scout's room basically the same and probably hers as well. The house has three bedrooms, so I'll take the third."

"That's really nice of you." Betsy wasn't sure why the idea of Violet living so close gave her warm fuzzies, but she couldn't stop the smile. "Do you know when you'll be all moved in?"

"Probably in the next few days. Transports are the best for that, don't you think?"

They started walking toward the door. "Yes. Moving any other way is barbaric." Betsy said this with feeling. She'd moved too many times the old-fashioned way. "So, dinner. How about we find a nice ramen restaurant? I could use something homey."

"Oh, that sounds great." Violet nodded.

Since Violet had transported to the going-away event, Betsy drove them to the restaurant. As they drove, she pointed out some of the main highlights of the city, giving Violet a small, guided tour. She selected a restaurant downtown, so they got to see the capital and where Betsy worked.

"Everything is so pretty here. Thanks for showing me all of this."

Betsy hooked her arm through Violet's. "Any time you want." Not only did the connection of their arms feel right, but the small fireworks of shivers that shot through her body surprised her.

Was that a tremble in Violet's arm too? Is she feeling this as well? Gah, why am I acting like a girl a quarter my age?

She suddenly realized Violet had asked her something. "I'm sorry, what did you say?"

Violet chuckled ... and it was delightful. "How long have you lived around here? I know you move around."

"In Madison? I think it's been about thirty years. Maybe more. Moving is a pain, and I do love my current house. I don't love the snow."

"Do you live near the chanzii settlement?" Her blue eyes met Betsy's, sparkling in the twilight, a small smile playing across her face.

"I'm not far, but no, not that close." They had to avoid cars as they crossed the street. "I know you'll be spending the next couple of days moving. Maybe you can come out and visit sometime."

"I'd like that."

They walked for a bit, looking at the sites of downtown Madison. When they got to the restaurant, the host sat them right away. After looking over the menu, they each selected a ramen bowl and decided to share some barbecue pork bao buns as an appetizer.

Betsy leaned back. "I need to know how much you want to participate in the next few weeks."

Violet's eyes widened. "What do you mean?"

"Well, do you want to join me at the press conferences? Come with me when I go into the government agency in New York? They're hoping I'd have someone, specifically an alien, who could help answer questions. As the top chanzii representative, you're now their liaison, right? Since you've been on-planet for two years, you know about as much as any of us about how things work around here."

Violet started to laugh. Betsy narrowed her eyes. "What?"

"You could always take Xantay."

"Gods above, can you imagine? She doesn't know how to filter." Betsy smiled back at Violet. "Not to mention, we'd have to somehow get these language translators to every person on the planet." She tapped her earpiece. "Otherwise, everyone would just hear the qynad growling and roaring. I mean, it'd be fun ... but unproductive."

"Yeah." Violet slumped. "So much for that idea." She rubbed her neck. "We should carry a stash of the translating earpieces with us now that she's on-planet. Though we can't easily provide for everyone ... not yet, we'll need to ensure everyone she interacts with has them."

"That's an excellent point." Betsy waved her spoon at Violet, narrowing her eyes. "You're smart. So, press conferences?"

A smile spread across her face. "Yes. I'm all in. However you need me."

One brow rose. "However, huh?"

Violet laughed. "You know what I mean."

"We'll circle back to that one later."

"Ha." Violet ate one of the bao buns, her whole face alight with amusement. "Now, besides this future meeting with the government people—"

"Monday."

"Monday?"

Betsy nodded. "Yep, meetings on Monday or Tuesday, depending on schedules, and press conferences on Thursday."

"Okay, so anything else on your list of demands?"

Smiling wide, Betsy thought it over. "I have weekly meetings with the Pillars and a town of magic users ... besides that, you know, relaxing by the pool with my new ven."

Violet laughed. "Oh, is that all? Sounds like a breeze. Well, count me in however I can help. Except the ven. You're on your own with them."

Betsy laughed. She had a feeling having this chanzii liaison around would keep her on her toes.

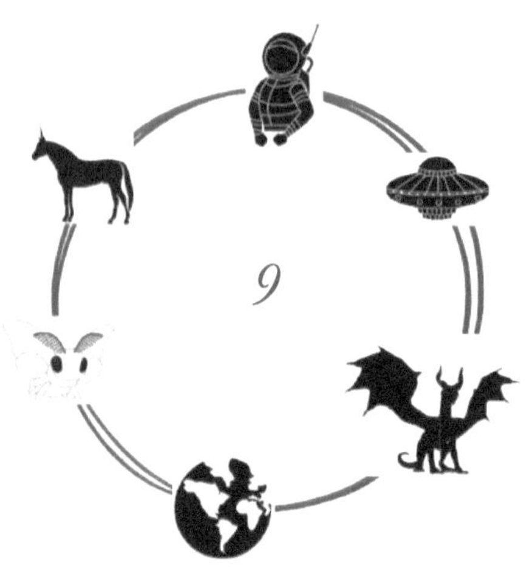

9

Top Brass

Violet

On Saturday, after everyone returning to Abritos left, and while Violet and Betsy celebrated her promotion, a group from Soaring Arbor Heights came in to remove everything from Thorn's house—save Thorn's and Scout's bedrooms. Once that was done, they painted. Violet left detailed notes on the panel about what she wanted done.

The main living room was terracotta, and someone had painted a rainbow of flowers along the border of the top of the room. They painted her bedroom cream with one accent wall a deep eggplant. The kitchen's cabinets were all natural wood, so she'd told the crew to leave the white walls and stone backsplash. She gave the same direction in the bathroom, with the stylized black, gray, and white subway tiles. She didn't see any reason to change any of it.

After dinner with Betsy, she'd returned home to Seattle for one last night. On Sunday morning, when she got to the house, the place smelled like paint, but everything looked amazing and exactly how she'd envisioned it. Violet had spent all day getting her belongings set up.

She didn't have much to unpack. Two of her friends from the neighborhood came to help her move things around and hang up paintings. By early evening, the place felt like home.

Waking up Monday morning, she felt excited for this new chapter in her career. Ever since she could remember, she'd wanted to be an explorer, someone who experienced different worlds and cultures. She hated what the krottel had done to her world, but now that she'd been forced to leave, she wasn't sure she'd ever return.

Part of her loved Earth. She knew the planet was backward in many ways compared to Abritos, but it also had an energy she enjoyed. She hoped she could convince whatever new government her world elected to allow her to continue to represent them. If not, she may try to remain with whatever type of green card the planet created for aliens.

Don't leave the pedesterizer before you put on the breaks, Violet! Ensure you like this new position ... what if you and Betsy don't work well professionally? She smiled, imagining her home world's transportation vehicle on Earth. Somewhere between a car and a bicycle, she wasn't sure humans had the muscle or stamina for a pedesterizer, but she missed them. They would've made traveling in the rain less sloppy.

The meeting with Betsy and the government officials would start at ten New York time—Eastern Standard. Betsy agreed to meet at Violet's place at half past eight so they could transport together.

Since Wisconsin was Central Standard, they were an hour behind.

Sitting in the kitchen, Violet sipped her coffee and finished a bowl of oats with fruit. She did miss some of the food from back home, but the odd flavors of Earth were beginning to grow on her. She even debated taking a cooking class.

A knock on her door jolted her from her thoughts of food and cooking, though the new thought of Betsy at her door made her smile. She put her dishes in the sink, smoothed out her spring dress, and opened her home to Betsy.

She stood there in a pair of high-waisted, flared, green, flood pants and a short-sleeved navy-blue top. Her sandy-blond hair was pinned back, the waves hanging just past her shoulders. Violet met her gray eyes, hoping the other woman didn't notice her checking her out.

"Hi, Betsy. Did you have breakfast?" A smile spread slowly across Violet's face. She loved that she'd be working with this Pillar. Any of them would be an honor, but Betsy ... gah! She felt like she was acting like a school r'grazz.

"I did. Are you all moved in already?" She gazed around Violet to look into the living room.

"We have a bit of time. We could check out the building. I could show you around there, or you can let me see how you changed this house to be your own."

Warmth filled Violet. "Come, let me show you what we did. I've only changed a few things, really." She clasped Betsy's hand and tingles traveled up her arm. With a small smile, she led the other woman into the living room.

Sounding awed, Betsy said, "Whoa! When did you have time to paint and redecorate? This is fantastic! I didn't know you were so artistic."

"Ha." The thought was ridiculous. "I'm not. But others around here are. The painting was done on Saturday during our date ... I mean, our tour and meal."

A slow smile spread across Betsy's face, almost taking Violet's breath away. "We can call it a date if you want. Though, on Earth, a date usually ends with a kiss." She leaned down and brushed her lips against Violet's. "There, now it's official. We had a first date." Betsy's cheeks were bright red, making Violet feel better about her own nerves.

"First, huh? Are you expecting more?"

With a slight shrug, Betsy waggled her brows. "Maybe."

Violet laughed. "Okay, let me continue the tour." She spun on her heel before her head exploded from the conversation. "I didn't change anything in the kitchen except the table. I had my own, and I preferred it. The only other big change is the group painted the room I'm staying in."

Betsy ducked her head in. "Oh! I love the accent wall. No flowers? Or a tree?"

"I think they ran out of time. I'm thinking of heading downtown and buying more artwork. There were some amazing shops."

"Sounds like a plan." Betsy seemed pleased with everything. Not that her approval was needed, but it made Violet happy. "Shall we head to our appointment?"

"Certainly."

In the kitchen, Betsy entered the command into the panel, and a moment later, they were in an alcove on the ground floor of the government building.

With a sigh, Betsy shook her head. "I've asked them to put a landing spot on the correct floor, but they say security could be compromised. So we are stuck down here."

"I hate to say this, but on Abritos, it's the same way. I know right now the only people transporting are safe, but now that everything is out … or coming out, having the right protocols in place isn't necessarily bad."

Betsy snorted. "You sound like Orson."

They walked through security and toward the elevators. "Honestly, I've had worse insults."

The elevator whisked them up quickly, and the doors opened into a light and airy reception area. A woman with short brown hair and brown eyes narrowed them before recognizing Betsy, then her face transformed. "Ah! Ms. Doeth, you're early. I can have coffee or tea brought in for you." She started typing on the computer. "And this is Major North representing the chanziian people?"

Violet had to lock her jaw shut to stop it from hanging open. She'd just been promoted over the weekend. Chills played throughout her body thinking about the promotion. It wasn't that she didn't think she deserved it. She just hadn't been working toward it … not yet. She wasn't even two hundred years old.

"Yes. As always, you're on top of things, Miranda. I'd love coffee and maybe some muffins. Violet?"

She nodded. "Please, that sounds amazing."

The two headed down a hall and through a door. The far wall had windows overlooking the city. Down the center of the room was a huge cherrywood table. Betsy pointed them to some seats. As was her habit, Violet rubbed her hands on the underside of the beautiful furniture, and sure enough, there were slots for electronics to be charged. This was a dwarven-made piece of artwork.

It only took a couple of minutes for the door to open and two men to enter. Violet recognized the first. An older gentleman, by Earth's standards, with white hair and sparkling blue eyes. He looked like the kind of man who knew more than anyone in the room.

The other was a kid. He had dark auburn hair, blue eyes, and freckles. He barely looked old enough to be out of school. Though, by Earth's standards, he was probably well on his way to adulthood.

They sat, and Betsy smiled ... it wasn't one Violet would want to be on the other side of. "Juk." Her smile softened. "Orson, this is Major Violet North. She will be working with me now that Commander Firoza is returning to oversee the rebuilding of Abritos."

Orson nodded. "Excellent. Welcome to the Department of Interstellar Coexistence and Knowledge Sharing! We're glad to have you."

Violet's eyes widened as she looked from Orson to Juk to Betsy and back to Juk. Finally, she swung her head to Betsy and half-covered her mouth. "Do they know their department's acronym spells out DICKS?"

Orson laughed, and Juk's brows came together, confused. He said, "What? No. That's not ..."

"We let Betsy do one thing ..." Orson sighed as if a committee had spent hours making a decision.

"Oh, it's not even as if it were your decision. I named this department before you were even born. And even your predecessor liked to give me the young DICKS to train." She sighed dramatically as if put out ... which, thinking about it, she probably was.

Before Juk could say anything, because he looked ready to burst, Orson said, "Okay, so we now have two of you. Any chance of a third?"

"We could bring a qynad," Betsy suggested, one side of her mouth turning up in a smirk.

Violet laughed, imagining the growling sounds everyone without an earpiece would hear. An utter disaster. She thought about the meeting on the Ziner the previous week, where the whole room had been wired and magicked to allow everyone to understand the language spoken. No earpieces needed.

With a sigh, she reached into her bag and found two translation devices. "I have a gift for my new friends." She slid them across the table.

Orson shook his head. "I have a set, but thanks."

Juk raised an eyebrow. "I believe I have some of these as well."

Betsy sighed. "You don't. You really need to finish reading those files you claimed to have read, pretty boy. And when a gorgeous alien offers you a gift, for all that is holy, take it. I know Orson didn't, but he's about to head back home. You're going to be around here. Do better."

Violet bit her cheek to ensure she didn't show the amusement she felt. Orson didn't even try. He slapped Juk on the back. "Listen to her, boy, and you'll never be led astray."

10

Let's Give a Prayer For Health

Betsy

They spent another hour in the conference room trying to guess the questions that could be asked at the press conference on Thursday. Despite all his annoying qualities, Juk did come up with some good ideas. Betsy knew how she wanted to answer most of them, though

Orson had some limitations on the amount of information shared.

Once they'd finished, Betsy and Violet headed out to find a deli to get lunch. Violet gazed around the city. "I love it here. It's been a long time since I've had reason to visit Manhattan."

"Well, we'll be here at least once a week while we're doing the press conferences. And on Thursday, we have a press conference. It's at three London time, which is nine in the morning for us. We can leave at seven and meet up with Zuza and get a proper lunch—brunch?—before we're on the international stage."

"Oh! That sounds great. I hadn't even considered these press conferences translated into meals all over the world." Her voice got a far-off, distracted tone.

"Consider it payment for the questions we'll have to answer and dealing with Juk. You do know that those won't be fun."

"I don't know. We'll have a galaxy of answers to give. It could be a ton of fun."

Betsy just gave her a side-eye. No one should be that happy about a press conference.

As much as Betsy enjoyed her time with Violet, she had a meeting with the other Pillars at three. They'd agreed to meet regularly to discuss both the press conferences and what they discovered during their research.

Kafi had asked for this meeting.

Since Betsy had driven to Violet's place, she decided to head to her downtown office after they returned to Wisconsin. She arrived a bit early and finished up some paperwork. She'd fantasized about splitting off some of the piles of paperwork and giving them to Viera, but now her friend was gone.

Oh, well. I've done all this work by myself for years. I guess I can continue to do it.

At just before three, she logged onto her computer and started the encrypted program that let her and the other Pillars speak privately. When her box popped up on the screen, she saw Zuza, his perfectly put-together outfit clear on the monitor and his blue eyes sparkling with a smile. Next to him, Kafi's mischievous, boyish face made Betsy wonder if she'd missed a joke. His dark eyes crinkled at the side and his dark hair fell forward as he leaned in as if he were about to say something when Ania's box appeared.

"Afternoon, everyone … except you, Ania. Morning." Betsy leaned down to her small refrigerator and grabbed a soda.

Ania yawned, her reddish-orange hair a mess and her green eyes drooping. "Nah, I haven't slept, mate. Long night. Just waiting for the meeting to end, and then I'll sleep."

While she spoke, Marco finally showed up. "Wild, Ania! Or at your age, do you only sleep once every two or three days?" His brown hair was disheveled, and he looked ready to stretch out and play a video game.

"Boy!" she snapped. "Don't think I can't find you and teach you a thing or two."

Marco laughed.

Zuza smirked. "She may be able to stay up for a week at a time, but I need my beauty sleep. I'm not this pretty without my shuteye. Now, Kafi, talk."

He nodded, then looked down. "I've spent the last few days researching the religious sects both online and by traveling. I got to some spots around here, Ghana, but also visited Nigeria, Sudan, and down to Botswana and South Africa. I debated a few other spots but stuck to where I have friends I could visit who own land with woods. It helps with transportation."

"That's a good variety of spots." Zuza was gazing down. It looked like he was taking notes. "So, what did you find?"

Kafi's face was grim. "Well, that's just it. I feel some of this we should've found before. There were three leaders, one each in the Sudan, Botswana, and South Africa. I found them because they were being really loud. Anyway, these religious leaders were telling people they could heal with the laying of hands."

Ania shook her head. "Isn't this the same claim that has been made for years?"

"Yes, but this time, I went to each of their 'presentations.' I could feel the magic in the air. My only guess is these people were using a combination of life and gas. In each case, they healed three to four people, using the healing as proof that God loved them, and they had the hand of God. They then went on to preach."

Betsy thought about her flavor of magic over that of the three interlopers who had made her look like an international fool. Wizards, outside of Elders, had two proficiencies. Except for the rare few, probably ninety to ninety-five percent of the galaxy had sensing or life. How Viera ended up with time was a real mystery. And then imbuement, the dying proficiency. Within the Pillars, they all had life, except for Zuza, who had sensing.

The second proficiency was elemental. These were evenly split across the galaxy, though the Pillars on Earth only had gas, liquid, and solid. None had energy.

Not having the proficiency didn't mean a practitioner old enough couldn't tap into the other magics. It just took time and effort and often left the person drained.

Kafi spoke, pulling Betsy from her thoughts. His voice took on a vibrato as if he were one of the preachers. *"Have you seen the evils happening in the United States of America? Those heathens who are consorting with aliens. Their sins were present in their ability to touch the devil's soul. Seduced by him to use magic. We here in God's land know that our simple life, without the aliens and whatever their slick serpent tongues may promise, is the right path."*

Betsy saw sneers and looks of annoyance in all the monitor boxes, including hers. Kafi sighed. "As the crowd cheered, I moved on to the next venue. In the end, they all pretty much gave the same message."

Betsy rubbed her face. "Do you think these people have been using magic, like Oz, for some number of years, or do you think this is a new development?"

"I don't know." Kafi slumped. "That's the next thing on my list. I just wanted to get what I found on all of your radars. We know Oz has a town of people using imbuing magic. Well, we have a few people healing around Africa."

"Oz is on my shortlist. I'll be getting there once I have the press conferences figured out." Betsy leaned back, thinking about how long her to-do list kept getting.

In his box, Zuza shook his head. "That should be a low priority, in my opinion. We need to speak with them, but they've obviously been around for years, possibly centuries, and they aren't going anywhere. From what you said, they aren't about to go to the media. We need to get ahead of what will spread first."

Ania's face scrunched up in disgust. "I agree. Don't drop them from the list but focus on the larger world first." She sighed. "I'll do more digging around Australia. Then I'll move to Asia and Europe."

Marco nodded. "There are a few conspiracy groups online, but nothing we didn't expect. Nothing that shows danger or actual magic."

Zuza nodded. "Same for academia. You know them, they don't tend to move very fast. Once their decisions have gone through a few levels of checks and balances, then we'll know what form of annoyance they bring."

"Okay, keep up the good work." Betsy mentally cataloged all the news. She knew she should take some notes, but she wanted these notes at home. She knew she could remember what needed to be written down once she got there. "We'll talk after the next press conference. It's in London, so I'll be with Zuza. Unless there's reason to send her home separately, Major North will be in the room listening in."

The others leaned in. Ania's smile returned. "Violet was promoted?"

"She was. Right before Thorn left. She'll be our liaison from here on out. She also moved into Thorn's house, so she's closer to the chaos." Betsy's mind played over the kiss she'd playfully given the other woman. She wasn't sure why she'd done it, but it warmed her to think about it.

The meeting ended with a general sense of happiness.

Responsibilities

Betsy

Tuesday morning, Betsy decided to delay heading into her office to play with the ven. Her home was new to them, and she wanted the beasts to be comfortable. It was time for them to learn the boundaries of her property.

After breakfast, she took Wesley, his black fur glistening, and Buttercup, sparkling gray with black markings, out to the woods. Their antennae vibrated with excitement as their heads darted left and right, taking in their new environment.

"Let's learn our boundaries, my baby friends." The two were barely old enough to be separated from their mom, but Thorn had been happy to not take five baby ven back to Abritos with her. Betsy started to jog, following a trail that wound through the trees that filled her property.

The two ven flew around her, dipping and spinning, chirping in delight. In the sun, Buttercup's gray fur almost glowed an iridescent silver. It reminded Betsy of her last visit to Abritos years ago when she first saw ven flying free in the trees. Wes disappeared into the shadows, a void in her vision.

As she ran, Betsy felt the burn in her muscles. It had been a while since she'd let herself move and stretch. The last few months had been filled with so much work that she hadn't had time to focus on relaxation.

With the invasion of the krottel and the subsequent information explosion of aliens and magic all over the planet, Betsy knew her days of leisure were numbered. Soon, she'd be one of a small part of people putting out fires worldwide.

Wes and Buttercup swooped down across her path, and she almost tripped over them. She decided to laugh versus swear at their antics.

There was a time when more Pillars and stronger magic wielders were available on Earth. As much as she respected Marco and Kafi, they were young. Marco was just over eighty. He hadn't even spent much time off Earth and barely knew anything about other aliens.

I know this is part of what we trained for, but Gods above, why now? Would a few more centuries have been too much to ask for? Maybe at a time when we had more than five Pillars?

And then there was Ania. Over six hundred. *Is she going to have a child? Will she be the last of her line? Or Zuza? Will we drop to four Pillars, or will everything change with the knowledge of magic? How did we all get to be so old without kids?*

There were so many questions and Betsy both feared and was excited for the answers.

After she got home and showered, she let the ven decide where they wanted to spend the day. It didn't surprise her when they opted for outside. It was more space and new to them. The same wards that kept strangers out should keep the rascals in and safe.

She had another snack, then transported to her office. There were so many files to organize. She spent a couple of hours catching up on odd jobs.

Having an office on State Street meant there were a ton of options for lunch. She went out, got a pasta bowl, and brought it back for a working lunch, eating while she cleared off a full quarter of her desk.

Productivity, thy name is Betsy!

Halfway through the food, her phone rang. "Betsy Doeth speaking."

"Oh, Betsy, excellent. It's Mrs. Kor, um, Tammy Kor, oh, I mean, just Tammy. You know, Viera's mom?"

"Hi, Tammy. Can I help you with something?"

She sighed. "Yes, dear. I was hoping I could ask a big favor of you."

The number of things on her list kept growing, but what was one more thing? "What do you need?" She tried to sound chipper.

"It's Viera's house. We found a realtor, and they found a buyer, but we don't know if we can trust someone to go through and do all of the walk-throughs and be our representative. You know how it is. There are so many scammers these days. Viera trusted you. We were hoping you could represent our—Viera's—interests."

Betsy slumped. She couldn't blame them. "Yes, Tammy. I'd be happy to help. Send over any forms you need me to sign."

"Do you have a fax number?"

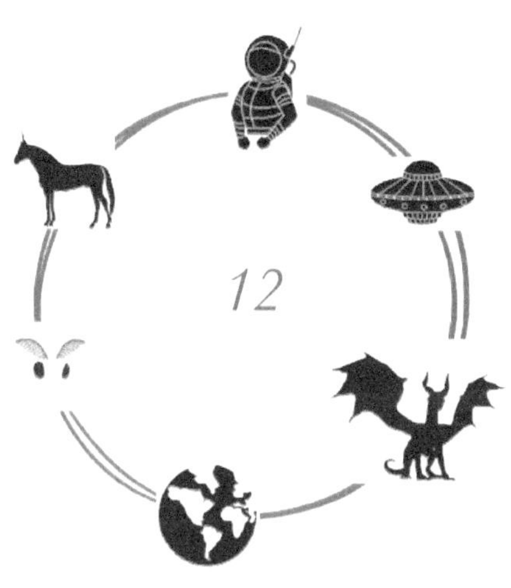

12

Message in a Bottle

Viera

The main promenade of Torville Station Number Six was just as full of beings as Viera remembered. Sitting in a café, she gaped as she saw new beasts roaming the large domed common area. Leaning over, she whispered to Thorn, though no one would be able to hear her,

"Is that a very large family of cats wearing leathers at that table, or small leopards?"

Thorn swung her head around. "Oh! I can't believe there are kucing on the station. They are such homebodies. They rarely head off-planet. Not since their war with the anjing about three or four hundred years ago that led to the destruction of one of the Torville Stations."

Viera narrowed her eyes at Thorn. "How many of these stations are there, and are there other space stations besides Torville stations?"

A low chuckle preceded Thorn's soft kiss. "I always forget how little you know. Torville is a family name—or at least used to be. They currently have eight stations up and running in this quadrant. Several families run stations, but the most reputable three are Torville, Q'olrit, and Zy'Boon. Those three families have twenty-nine stations scattered about the most populated areas."

"And this is the closest one to Earth?"

"Yes. Though, now that—"

"Good morning, Commander, Elder and newest Pillar of Earth. It is a great honor to see you both this morning." Viera smiled wide at the deep baritone voice that practically vibrated her bones as

Balzeno the dwarf approached them. Whereas most dwarves never left their planet, he traveled, experiencing the universe. Despite Balzeno's spry movements, Viera knew he had to be the oldest being she'd met to date. He always made a point of calling her Elder because she had three proficiencies despite only having magic for a few months so far. A weird accident that happened because of how the krottel awakened her magic. As with last time, his thick hair was pinned back, allowing his green eyes to twinkle in the station's light. "May I join you?"

Viera was dumbfounded that such a prestigious Elder would want to join them and could barely get her mind to work. Thankfully, Thorn had more wits about her. "Of course, Elder Balzeno. It would be our pleasure to host you this morning for breakfast."

Once he sat, Viera smiled and had to say, "I should tell you, I'm not technically a Pillar of Earth any longer ... I don't think. I'm headed off to Abritos with Commander Firoza."

His eyes twinkled, and then he faced Thorn. "Host, smost! I just want to enjoy some food with pleasant company. And since I saw you, I thought we could share some news. And look at that, you've already started. Excellent to hear some of the chanzii are returning, and with an Elder, no less."

My God! He's a gossip! Viera controlled her giggles but not the smile that spread across her face. "Well, what information do you have to share? Because I believe we have something else to share, something big."

Thorn narrowed her eyes at Viera, but she knew what she was doing. Before leaving Earth, she and Betsy had discussed how much to tell about Earth's newest town. They'd decided it was time to let others know. It would get out regardless of what they did, and if some key players they chose knew, then at least Betsy knew good aliens would control the information, not just the scoundrels.

"Well, I don't so much have galactic news as a gift, youngling." He reached into a small side pouch that sat just over his hip. It looked like a money bag from mythical D&D campaigns and amused Viera. She wondered if he'd give her another imbued item. She had three, and what she had didn't always seem to get along ... if one could describe imbued items as relating to each other that way.

The server approached then, placing the plates of food Thorn had ordered in front of them. One of her biggest goals over the next year was to learn enough Galactic Standard to order her own food. She debated stealing a menu but then thought Scout could probably recreate one for her.

When she looked back at Balzeno, he had a book—a *tome!*—in front of him on the table, though he faced the server, ordering his own food. The ginormous book was the size of a notebook, at least a standard piece of paper, but it was *thick*. She wanted to get out a ruler but feared it was as tall as any ruler she might carry.

God above, that thing has to be at least twelve inches thick. And where the hell did he carry it? There's no way it was in that tiny bag on his hip.

She shook her head, then snapped her mouth shut as soon as she realized it was hanging open.

"—else?"

"No," Thorn snorted, then elbowed her. "I think this will be good for me. Viera, do you need anything? More coffee? You seem a bit dazed."

"Um ..." Viera searched the table and realized her mug was empty. "Yes, more coffee, please." She thought back on the conversation with Thorn.

"Do all the space stations have coffee or just this one?"

"Only the Torville stations. They have a contract with the Pillars. It was made with Gandalf about two hundred—"

"Three hundred twenty-seven years ago," Balzeno interrupted. "Best move they ever made. They were floundering, especially after that silly war. After their third station was destroyed about five hundred and sixty years ago, that piece of the galaxy was full of bandits. Though they never built a new station, they did have storage and one of their main resource planets there. They bled money trying to secure it. The family needed money. What Gandalf demanded was expensive, but I tell you, exclusive rights to coffee was a genius move. They've updated it a few times. In the last century or so, they've added tacos, sushi, bratwurst with sauerkraut, macaron cookies, vegemite, and jollof rice."

Viera smiled. "They got food from all over the planet. I understand all of that except the vegemite."

"What?" Both Thorn and Balzeno sounded offended. Balzeno spoke first. "That's a crowd favorite. It's used on everything." He pointed to a small jar a server put on a table near them. "It's a bit expensive, but it's great on just about everything."

A shiver ran down Viera's spine. She'd never liked the Australian spread. "Okay, that's amazing. So, tell me, what's that?" She pointed to the book.

"Oh, it's the user manual for your bracelet." One meaty hand patted the mountain of pages lovingly. "I knew I had it somewhere. I'm glad I ran into you and have it to hand over. I debated heading to Earth to give it to you, though I know the planet is closed."

"It's ... no, I'll explain in a moment." Viera waved her hand at the object that could be a library all in itself. "That? That will teach me to use this?" She gently stroked the small silver piece of artwork around her wrist. The two interwoven bands with leaves or small silver flowers at the juncture points. She never had figured out how to take the thing off *or* how it worked.

Elder Balzeno had given her the bracelet and with Flower Prancer's help, she was trying to learn how to use it. Gazing at the huge book, she didn't feel as bad for not mastering the finer details of the imbued item.

"Why, yes. If you read the first nineteen or so zods, you'll learn the basics of the bracelet. There is a lot in there, so you don't want to skip any of it, but the beginning is important. Oh, and the last two and a half to three zods as well. Those should be read right away as well."

"Can't you speak in a standard unit!" Flower Prancer's sharp tones barely preceded the clomping of his hooves across the restaurant. He was followed by Horax and Scout, both moving with much more stealth and grace. "Is this how the whole book is written, Elder?"

The way the yonat said "Elder" didn't sound like a compliment.

Scout reached over to take the book. "Mom, if you can order for me, I'll take this back to the room and be back really quick. This book looks amazing. And, Ms. Kor, I can help you with zods. They're a bit obscure, but not as bad as Flower Prancer is making it out."

Thorn reached over and ruffled the boy's hair. "Sure, hurry back."

"Have they told you about the imbuers?" Flower Prancer's tail swished with his annoyance.

The dwarf's eyes widened. "The what?"

If Viera could figure out how to shoot laser beams from her eyes, she'd knock the silly yonat off his podium of self-importance. With a sigh, she explained what happened first with the krottel, then the press conference, and finally, the new magical community on Earth. "I can't tell you more. We left right after we learned about this town. Pillar Doeth and the others are planning on doing the investigation in the next week or so ... um, probably seven to ten days, I would guess. With what the krottel did, their first priority is the larger Earth's population."

While she spoke, the server returned, and the new orders were put in.

A joyous smile spread on the dwarf's face. "So, does this mean there will be a time in the future when you'll be accepting liaisons to that closed-off planet of yours?"

Viera shrugged. "I'd suggest sending a message to Pillar Doeth or one of the others. I'm heading to Abritos with Thorn. I'm very much out of the loop. But I know there are three liaisons there now if you count Toby."

Flower Pracer scoffed. "No one counts him. Besides scaring humans into believing in Big Foot, the fing doesn't play a role in intergalactic politics. He just hides on Earth producing huckleberry pastries."

Scout ran up, interrupting anything more they'd say. "Mom, Mom! You'll never believe what we received."

"Breathe." She wrapped him in a hug. "Now, tell me what."

"It's Tiffany, Mom. She sent me a message." He started to bounce. His whole body was so full of joy that it slammed into Viera in full force. "Her parents want to visit Abritos!"

They Walk Among Us

Betsy

Wes and Buttercup flew around Betsy's house as she drank her coffee and tried to wake up. It was just after six ... noon in London, and she'd already showered and dressed. Ever since the krottel attack, Betsy hadn't been able to find a lot of downtime. She wished she didn't have to look to such an early hour to be awake, hang out with the ven, and relax.

"Okay, you two insane creatures, inside or out today? It's going to be a long day, and I may not return until tomorrow. I know you like to hunt and there's an auto-feeder in the barn ... so, the freedom of the woods?"

The oversized, fluffy moth-like creatures darted between Betsy and the door. She had no idea why Thorn didn't love the ven. They were the best creatures in just about the entire galaxy, in Betsy's opinion. She'd wanted one ever since she saw one during her first trip to Torville Station Number Four. That station was close to the vens' home planet, and there were a lot of them there. The aliens who sold them always had a ton flying around the promenade.

At that time, because that station was so far from Earth, her grandfather told her it would be impossible. Thinking back now, she was pretty sure it was because hiding the ven on Earth would've been hard, not the distance the station had been from Earth.

Well, look at me now! I have two, you crazy man!

With a sigh, Betsy realized it was getting late. She knew she had to schedule time to relax at home. Her wards were based on the time she spent there, and all this traveling around the world would weaken them. It wasn't an immediate worry but something she had to consider.

Betsy put her coffee in a travel mug and headed to her car. She needed to get to Violet's house so they could travel to Zuza's flat in London together. He promised to take them out to breakfast, his lunch, and then over to the location of the press conference that was being held today.

There were few cars on the road this early in the morning, and the drive to Violet's didn't take long. Betsy grabbed her purse and walked to the door, excitement at seeing Violet bubbling inside her. She knew she shouldn't be this happy about the chanziian major, but their flirting had opened a side of Betsy she'd tucked away years ago ... decades? It felt nice feeling tingles for someone again.

Once she knocked, it didn't take long for Violet to answer. As always, the petite woman looked amazing with her blond hair pulled back in a ponytail and a perfectly appropriate blue dress for the day.

I was lucky to find clean pants and a shirt to throw on.

"Betsy, you're early. Do you think Zuza will mind if we show up now?" Her eyes sparkled, and she blushed after looking Betsy up and down. It warmed Betsy to her soul.

"Probably not. It's almost noon there, but we'll call first."

They headed to the panel in the kitchen, and Betsy sent a message to Zuza. He replied right away that he was eagerly ready and waiting.

A few moments later, the world melted around them as they transported to London.

Zuza stood in front of them in gray slacks and a tucked-in black button-down shirt. He smiled in welcome. "Welcome to London, Major North."

"Oh, thank you, Pillar Brzezinki. It is an honor to be invited into your home." She gazed around his study lined with walnut bookcases stained dark, full of books that looked as old as they actually were. "But do call me Violet. There's no reason for such honorifics between friends, right? We can be friends, can't we?"

His smile widened. "I would like that. But you must call me Zuza."

The three headed out to a local pub to get a meal. Afterward, Zuza showed them to the venue where they would be holding the press conference.

"How many aliens are there?"

Betsy and Violet sat at a table in front of several dozen press and spectators. Cameras and translators lined the room. A local news celebrity, Bobby Tonts, hosted the event.

"Please hold all questions," Bobby said with a million-dollar smile. "I'd like to introduce to you Betsy Doeth and Violet North. I'm going to start by explaining a few things I have just learned. Betsy Doeth, one of the original contacts between us and the aliens, as well as a magic wielder, is known as a Pillar. If you want to address her, please do so by Pillar Doeth. It is her respected title. As for Violet North, she is a major for the chanziians. You can refer to her as Major North."

The crowd started mumbling and writing on their pads or speaking into devices. Betsy smiled, trying not to forget the cameras pointed at her and Violet. "Thank you, Mr. Tonts. We appreciate you having us and giving us space to answer the questions many people have." She turned to the crowd and cameras. "Major North and I plan on having these conferences every Thursday. You can check the website on the flyers provided or at the bottom of the screen if you're watching. It's also linked through the QR code."

Bobby's glowing smile showed up one more time, nearly blinding Betsy. "We'll be recording this event as well. You can rewatch it on our station, the affiliates, Pillar Doeth's website, and, I'm sure, any number of other sources. And now we can get to that first question." He waved his hand back toward Betsy and Violet.

And so it begins.

Betsy sent a small ironic shrug up to her dad. They'd always wondered what this day would look like. "There are a lot of alien races, as you can probably imagine. Up until now, Earth has had mostly closed borders. We've allowed a few in under very strict limitations."

A man with a gruff voice in the back asked, "Why were we attacked?"

"That's a longer answer." Betsy had known this was coming but had hoped this first press conference would focus on magic and not aliens. She knew there was a chance since both were human obsessions, but safety won out. "Magic is created by the beings living on a planet. Because we have such a large population and so few magical users, our planet is thick with magical potential."

"So, we were attacked for our magical resource?" a woman near the back asked, her recording device held out.

"No," Betsy said, trying to make sure her voice was clear and she spoke slowly. She wanted everyone to understand the situation the first time. *Delusional much? When have the masses ever understood the first time ... or even the second?* "Despite our magical potential, our planet is protected by a larger governing body in the galaxy." She paused to let the idea of rules within the wild vastness of space sink in. "When the aliens that attacked approached, one of the few Earthbound government bodies that knew about aliens tried to contact them to ask their intentions. The aliens didn't understand our ways. They believed they'd been lied to. If this person was contacting them, a leader of the people, then obviously all the people of Earth must know about aliens."

"That's how it should've been!" a teen in the back yelled. Others began talking throughout the crowd, most agreeing with him.

Betsy waited, knowing that interrupting wouldn't help.

Bobby Tonts's laughter reverberated through the room. "Well, now, I don't know about all of you, but I'd like to hear more answers. We only have an hour. We can let this nice young man continue to voice his very valid opinion about a past we can't change, or we can move forward, getting our questions answered."

"Were the invaders punished? And who decided the punishment?"

Before Betsy could come up with an answer, knowing this was close to topics she and Orson didn't want covered, someone on the other side of the room shot to his feet. "Yeah, I was visiting Chicago and saw everything. Those invaders weren't just humanoids like you two. There were bugs too. Do we know we got them all?" He shivered before sitting back down.

Good. They don't know that the bugs and the humanoids were one and the same. One issue avoided.

"My people led the meeting that determined the punishment." Violet's face was hard, but she spoke clearly. "In that meeting were members of Earth's government, Earth Pillars, galactic Elders—those we consider the highest leaders—and leaders of my world, Abritos. The invaders who came here had previously invaded Abritos. If you remember from last week, my Commander discussed this. Unlike what happened on my planet, their invasion here was stopped. Different alien groups came together to stop them before they could get a toehold on your planet."

"Does that mean you brought the aliens here?" a man in the center of the group asked, interrupting her answer.

Betsy realized the question wasn't entirely incorrect. If the chanziian people weren't here, Viera wouldn't have been accidentally taken to Torville Station Number Six and kidnapped by the krottel. It was that chain of events which had led the bugs to find Earth, but no one was to blame for their actions but them.

Violet shook her head. "No. We've been here for several years. The krottel, the aliens who invaded, only just learned about Earth a few months ago. They are an alien race that needs magic to survive but doesn't create it themselves. During the meeting to determine what to do with them, since the ones you saw here are the last of their kind, they were sentenced to live out the rest of their lives on planets and no longer have access to space travel."

Though Betsy knew this sounded harsh to the room of questioners, she knew the final decision suited the krottel. The bugs had never wanted space travel. They preferred living underground. They just needed a planet with living beings to produce the magic. If they'd known that, many invaded planets and a lot of angst could've been avoided.

"And," Betsy said before anyone could interrupt, "we used a combination of magic and technology to scan the planet to ensure none were left behind. We are certain there are no krottel left on Earth."

A young girl, maybe early teens, raised her hand. Betsy pointed to her, though none of the others had been so polite. "Could I have already spoken to an alien before today? And if I run into one in the future, are there rules on how to engage with them?" Her voice was soft and full of wonder.

It warmed Betsy's heart seeing her. She was glad it had been decided to open these up to the public. Anyone could get a free ticket, first come, first serve, though half the seats were reserved for journalists. "I don't know if you've met an alien. My guess is probably not. There really aren't that many on the planet and they tend to find less populated places to live. In the next couple of years, however, Earth will evolve. The chanzii will head home once their planet has been rebuilt and is deemed safe. But now that Earth knows about aliens, I'm guessing many alien races will want to send a liaison or two to help build bridges of friendship. Major North is thinking about becoming one. The qynads have one here right now. They are the ones that look like dragons. As for more, we need to sit down as a world and decide."

In the stunned silence that followed her words, the same girl who'd spoken before raised her hand again but spoke before Betsy could signal her. "Are the dragons ... um, the, did you say qynad? Are they friendly?"

A wide smile spread over Betsy's face. "Yes, and the one here is very tech-savvy. I could bring her to one of these press conferences, but we'd all need language translators to understand her speech. The other option is creating a room with built-in translators, but that may take a bit more time. I'll see what we can do on our side."

That announcement caused more wide-eyed silence.

Then, the room erupted in questions.

All in The Name of Religion … or Science

Betsy

Though the aired part of the press conference only lasted an hour, it took them additional time to get out after answering all the questions, talking to the station staff, and filing a report for Juk.

Before they left, Betsy handed Violet a hat and sunglasses. One of Violet's brows lifted. "Do you really think this will help? People will know it's us as soon as we walk out of here."

Betsy smiled, hooked her arm through Violet's, and dragged her onto the bustling street. They were instantly one of many trying to get home after a long day. "What you're forgetting, dear friend, is that not everyone watched the press conference. More than that, no one expects to see us here, so we have a natural anonymity."

They got ice cream on the way back to Zuza's place to celebrate surviving their first on-air appearance. He hadn't stayed for the circus, stating he was going to head back to his flat and cook dinner.

"Okay, so what you're saying is, ice cream is on the docket at the end of each of these?"

"Absolutely." Betsy waggled her brows, trying not to think about Violet licking her ice cream. "I think we did a good job."

Violet nodded. "We did. And now everyone knows what to expect and should bring tougher questions."

Glaring, Betsy was amused to see Violet's shoulders shimmy with her mirth.

Once they finished their sweet treat, they slowly walked around, taking in the sights. Zuza had lived in London for years, and he lived close to several prime tourist spots. Violet had never seen Big Ben, the House of Parliament, or Westminster Abbey. They didn't bother with official tours. Seeing the outside of buildings and the mass of people was entertaining enough. Not to mention, Betsy loved visiting and seeing how things changed every time she came.

Violet stopped as a group of tourists swarmed past them. "What are your plans for the next few days?"

"I hope to visit that magic human town in Alabama ... Oz." Betsy felt heavy with all the things on her to-do list. She knew she should've made it to Oz before this, but the dissemination of information was a much higher priority.

"Is that really the town's name? Like, did it come before or after the movie?" Violet chuckled.

"You mean the book? There were books that came out at the turn of the century before the movie. I wonder if the town inspired the books which inspired the movie. Maybe someone who happened to have gone through the fair town of Oz and found inspiration."

Violet snorted. "Who knows. Though the movie centered around Kansas, not Alabama."

Betsy shrugged. "Maybe they ended up in Kansas and figured where the book centered didn't matter. They just liked the idea. Or they were trying to help hide the town. I have no idea. It's all in the past now."

"You should ask. Maybe use it as an icebreaker." The sassy tone in Violet's voice amused Betsy.

"Maybe I should. Though they may kick me out if I do."

"Some risks are worth taking, my friend."

They walked in silence for a few steps.

"So, are you going tomorrow?" There was something apprehensive or hopeful about Violet. Betsy wasn't sure what.

"No, I think Saturday. I'm hoping to catch more people home and available to talk. Since none of the people had cell phones, I'll have to go door to door." She cut her eyes over to Violet. "Why, were you thinking of something?"

They reached Zuza's place, and Betsy pushed the button to his flat.

Violet glanced up the side of the building. "I don't know. I enjoyed our first date ... though it wasn't official until after the fact." The door buzzed, and they headed in. "I was hoping we could try again. Maybe with Thai this time. It may be more date-like."

"Ah ... you're right. It probably was the ramen. Too casual. Thai would help a lot."

"My thoughts exactly." Violet smiled, her cheeks a bit rosy.

"I think dinner tomorrow would be lovely." Her heart beat a bit faster, and chills raced down her back.

What am I doing?

When they got to Zuza's floor, he waited by the open door. "We have about forty-five minutes before we need to log in for our call. I've made meat pies and garden peas. I hope you two are hungry."

Kafi sighed. "I focused on one of the towns. I moved in and got a job on a construction team. For the last four years, their current minister has been healing people who are free of sins, people he says are destined for the gates of heaven. People have been flocking to the area, so new homes have been popping up." He rubbed his face, then sipped from a mug. "When I sat in the back of his sermon ... or whatever ... he called up two people. One had a broken arm, a second had been healed the previous week—lung cancer. She'd gone to her doctor and was now cancer-free. The place went wild."

Ania's face scrunched up. "We need to get a copy of this woman's medical records. We also need to figure out how long this man has been healing. The people there have apparently always believed in the religious leader. Can we get a list of a few of his 'miracles?' Then do some hacking for medical backgrounds? Maybe put Juk on some of the computer work?"

Violet waved her hand, and Betsy smiled. She thought she had an idea of where this may be going. It was Zuza who spoke up, his voice amused. "As a reminder, we have Major North here. She has a suggestion, if everyone is okay with the interloper speaking."

There was a round of agreement, though Violet blushed. Room was made for Violet to be seen on camera. "Hi, everyone. I'm very sorry to bother the meeting. I just wanted to note that Xantay has recently come to Earth, and whereas Horax was good with computers and tech, she is a master. There's never been a computer that wouldn't give up its secrets to that qynad."

Marco smiled. "Oh, I like this idea. I haven't met her yet. Is she staying up on a ship, or has she found a place on-planet?"

"She's on the island." Betsy smiled. "I'm sure you could drop in and say 'hi.' I'm planning on checking up on her next week. And on a quick note, I'll be heading over to Oz on Saturday. We need to get a full sense of what these people are doing."

"Good." Ania slapped her hands down on the table. "I'm having a similar issue as Kafi." She leaned back, sneering. "The difference is the religious leader here is testing people to see if the sin outweighs the good. If it does, he sends the sinner down to Lucifer himself."

Everyone stopped moving. It looked like the feed froze. In a whisper, Betsy asked, "Did you just tell us he's killing people with magic?"

"That I did, mate. And the worst part, the majority don't pass. He only tests people who come to him after having done something awful to see if their souls have been cleansed after their atonement. As it goes, in most cases, they haven't done enough. Because of that, their families need to pay to save the souls of the rest of their motley crew."

Color had drained from many of the faces. "That's not how it works," Marco said in a quiet yet stern tone, disgust in his words. "Each person is judged for their own actions. I've studied the religions of many cultures. There's no paying for another's misdeeds."

"There is when the person testing the guilty can literally kill you with their test." Ania's voice was soft, sad, and pissed. "We need to find a way to stop him without making him a martyr."

While everyone spent a moment thinking about the horrors presented, Zuza cleared his throat. "In other news, there have been some reports out of academia. Scientists are asking for anyone showing signs of magic to come in for study and to help flesh out public information about what's going on. It's all above board, questions and answers, super safe sounding."

"Why do I feel like this won't end well?" Kafi mumbled under his breath. Betsy could only agree.

Zuza sighed. "I guess we'll just have to wait and see."

Du-Drop

Pearl

Five people milled about the store. It was almost lunchtime and Pearl's break. Though Mom was the mayor of Oz, she'd come at noon to take over, giving Pearl time to eat and visit Dulaine. The town was small enough that the mayor's office was only open in the mornings unless someone made an appointment.

"Pearl, I'm so glad you're home. We love having you back in town." Trent, one of Cassidy's dads, smiled at her as he approached the counter. "Cassidy told us all about your trip to New York. Being caught in that room with those people? I can't even imagine it."

"It was pretty intense, but you know me and Cassidy. I think Devlin had the worst of it."

Trent laughed. "Probably, left alone with the two of you." He handed her a couple of items he wanted to buy. "Do you know if your dad finished my special order?"

Spinning on her heel, Pearl slid the window open to Dad's workshop. "Dad, do you have Trent's—"

"Yes, yes, of course I do. I told him it would be ready today. Katz Apothecary always fulfills orders when promised." He got up and shuffled through piles on his workbench after repeating his standard line.

Pearl looked over to her area. "Is it that bag? Over there? On my desk?"

"Oh! Yes. I put it there for safety. I'm mixing up a tincture that's a bit ... explosive. You know. Don't want to harm the sold product."

With a sigh, she held out her hand so he could pass her Trent's bag. "Just remember, we don't really need any protection spells. The government isn't really coming to get us."

"That's fine, dear, but if they do, we'll be ready." Though he answered, he was already distracted by his work.

Pearl slid the window closed and gave Trent the bag. He smiled. "It makes him feel like he's doing something. It won't hurt anyone ... probably. And gives him something to do."

"You're right. Thank you." She smiled. Cassidy's dads had always been like second parents to her, and she respected what they said.

"Of course." He paid, then waved as he turned to walk to the door.

As he left, Mom came in. "Okay, Pearl, you have until two, maybe three. Go." She and Trent shook hands as they passed.

Pearl didn't need to be told twice. Her first stop was the bakery. "Hi, Maleah. Anything good for lunch?"

"I have a mushroom and leek galette." After Pearl nodded, she added, "Do you want a slice of flourless chocolate cake?"

"Yes, that would be wonderful."

"Are you picking up your family's order for fudge?"

As Pearl watched Maleah work behind the counter, she thought about the next few hours. "I'm going to go visit Dulaine after I eat. But I'll swing back after that."

"Sounds good. I'll put it on the family tab."

On the way to her sister, Pearl wanted to make a few other stops. After she ate, sitting in the park, she stopped at Clean And Inspire by Shenel.

Shenel was like everyone's cool aunt, and her store smelled amazing. "Afternoon, Pearl!" She narrowed her eyes. "You look tired. Come try some of my new lotion? It will help invigorate you. You know you need to come visit me to get a new blend every few months. Why have you neglected my store?"

"I've been away at college."

"That's no excuse, girl." She harrumphed.

The lotion smelled like the woods at Christmas. "This makes me want to have cookies and chocolate milk."

"You'll have to talk to Maleah about that. Just use this for the next two weeks, and we can speak afterward."

Pearl hugged her favorite shop owner. "What do I owe you?"

"If you don't leave right now, Ms. Pearl Katz, I'll swat your behind like the misbehaving child you're acting. Now, go!"

Laughing, Pearl headed out. Across the street, she found Trent behind the counter. "Are you following me? Did your dad give me the wrong bag?"

"No." Pearl's smile widened. "I'm here for your daughter."

"God above, yes! Please, take her."

"Dad! You're the worst. Well, you and Pops both are! I can't believe you." Cassidy came through a door from the back and kissed Trent on the cheek. "I'll be back in an hour or so." She shot Pearl a look, who nodded.

"We're going to go entertain Dulaine for a bit."

Trent sighed. "That poor girl. I can't imagine not having the ability to do any magic. She seems to be taking it in stride, but your parents ... They hide it well, but I can tell they're stressed. Your mother and I have been good friends for too long for me not to be able to read her."

Pearl didn't respond. It was a family matter and as much as she loved her best friend's parents, and as well as Trent may know Mom, she wouldn't spread stories about her own family.

Cassidy slapped her dad's arm. "Stop, you're embarrassing me now. I'll be back."

The two headed out. Dulaine wasn't in a school, really. Pearl's parents had hired a private tutor to work with her to help bring out her natural abilities with magic. If nothing manifested by her thirteenth birthday, that would be it. They had two years.

There were no records showing magic would or could appear in a person older than twelve, but her family would push for one extra year.

Pearl's parents found a one-room schoolhouse just outside of town where Dulaine's tutor, Kirke, could hold lessons. As the two walked down the street, they passed Devlin sitting at a small table outside his gem shop. "Hi, you two. Did you listen to the press conference on the radio or television yesterday?"

Cassidy scoffed. "No, why would we? I'm trying to forget everything about that whole fiasco." Her head tilted. "Though, was it that same person? Or did they bring in someone new to spread their stories?"

He sighed. "We can't bury our collective heads in the sand and hope it all goes away. You know that woman at the press conference? One of them, at least, or one of the others will show up here one day asking questions. They all thought magic was only used by five people on this planet. We have a full town. They're not just going to ignore us."

Pearl's shoulders drooped and her head fell back. "I know that, but I'd like to put off thinking about it or them until that inevitably happens. I love how our lives are and how our town works. They'll come and ruin it, but until then, we can enjoy our piece of utopia."

Devlin shook his head, disappointment written all over his stern face. "You shouldn't ignore the information they're spreading. Yesterday, it was about aliens. Next week, it could be about magic. We need to learn what they know. We shouldn't allow ourselves to remain in the dark."

"Fine," Pearl snapped. "When I get home, I'll log onto a computer and watch a rerun of the program."

Devlin's face hardened. "Did you just spend four years in college? Don't you understand technology any better?"

"Not really. When one can't be around it without it shorting out, one tends to ignore it."

"Ignorance doesn't look good on you, Pearl. Be better. You're going to be leading Oz one of these days." His tone didn't leave any room for argument. "But, yes, log in. They have a website. You can search for it. Watch what they had to say. And next week, Thursday, make sure you watch it live. We can't be caught unaware."

Even though Pearl knew he was right, she didn't want to think about the outside world right then. *I'm sure we have a few days, maybe even weeks. I'll talk with my parents when I get back to the store, see if they saw the press conference, get their take on the situation.*

After that, she and Cassidy finally made it to the school. The one-room schoolhouse sat at the edge of the woods. It was quiet and private and allowed

Dulaine time to learn indoors as well as plenty of room to run around outside.

Inside, Dulaine sat at a table on the side of the large room, drawing a picture. Kirke sat at her desk eating lunch. Pearl and Cassidy waved to the instructor and then sat with Dulaine.

"Hiya, sis, how are you doing today?"

Dulaine shrugged. "I still haven't made fire if that's what you're asking."

"No, I'm asking about *you*, silly."

The young girl sighed. She was only eleven but seemed to hold the weight of the world on her shoulders. Maturity wrapped around her like a cloak, squeezing tighter and tighter every day her magic didn't manifest.

Her gray eyes, so different from anyone's in town, finally gazed up at Pearl. "Kirke is worried about me. She's been teaching me the other school subjects, which are all easy, but she can't get me to do any kind of fire. If I can't do fire, why bother with anything else?"

Why, indeed. Has anyone ever tried anything else with her?

Pearl wrapped an arm around her sister. "Magic isn't the end of the world, Du-Drop. You will be an amazing person no matter what you can or can't do. You know that, right?"

She shrugged. "I can't do magic. I'm the only kid in town my age. I ... I don't know. I just wish there was more."

"I know. And one day, you'll think back on today and wonder what you'd ever been thinking."

A Bit of the Past

Betsy

"Were you on Abritos when the krottel attacked?"

The server brought them potstickers and crispy egg rolls for appetizers, as well as their Thai iced coffee.

"No, I'd left a few years earlier. I always knew I wanted to see the galaxy and different planets."

Betsy ate one of the potstickers, enjoying the burst of flavor. "Do you have family? I guess not back on Abritos, not yet. Your people are just now returning, but here on Earth or somewhere?"

The side of Violet's mouth twitched up. "I do, actually. Not on Earth. They ended up on other planets after the krottel forced the evacuation of everyone on Abritos. I have two younger sisters and an older brother. My parents died young in an accident." She waved her hand and rolled her eyes. "Long story. My brother ended up taking over the family farm. He was young at the time, sixty-three. But he loved it. He'd always wanted to be a farmer, and running the family business suited him."

"So, you used to be a farmer?" A slow smile spread on Betsy's face, imagining Violet tilling a field and feeding cows.

"Yes, well, no. My family farmed. And stop whatever it is you're envisioning. It's wrong. Our farms aren't like yours." Violet's smile turned genuine. She took a sip of her coffee and sighed. "You know, there isn't another planet that can match the coffee beans of Earth. They are the true magic of the galaxy." She chuckled.

"So I've heard. It saved the Torville family, from what I remember. Grandpa took me with him when he did his dealing."

Violet's eyes widened, finishing the bite of egg roll she'd taken. "I always forget you were *his* granddaughter."

Betsy groaned as she leaned back. "For years, he was a doddering old fool. Don't idolize him. Now, my dad. Did you ever meet him? Talk about amazing."

"Until coming here, I hadn't met anyone from Earth."

"And have we lived up to your expectations?"

She shrugged. "Maybe. I'm still on the fence about you, you know."

With a laugh, Betsy sipped her Thai iced coffee. "Enough of my family. Tell me about your siblings scattered all over the galaxy."

"Fine. But first, pre-krottel. Back to the farm. My sisters never wanted to live the rural life ... neither did I, as you can tell. Well, Ivory became a vet, so she's not too far from what we did as kids, but Faxon is like Viera, a teacher."

"Ivory, Faxon, Violet, and ... what's your brother's name?"

"Oh! Sorry, it's Onyx. When the krottel came, they all ended up on Jucinkt, the anjing home world."

"With the big cats? I didn't think they let anyone in." Betsy was shocked.

"When everyone on my planet had to leave, even Earth opened its borders. I'll admit, most of that was Commander Firoza. She single-handedly got more borders opened that no one thought would ever allow any of our people in. It's how a former baker is now the most powerful person on our world."

"Do you ever talk to them, your siblings? When was the last time you saw them?" Betsy felt sad for Violet out on the edge of the galaxy all alone. She knew that, on some level, this was what Violet wanted, but as more of her people left, would she begin to feel isolated and alone?

Violet smiled, and as always, it took Betsy's breath away. The woman was stunning in either version, her human costume or her natural skin. Just beautiful. *Focus, Betsy. She's talking!* "Yes, we used to have family group calls regularly, as our schedules permitted. We may be scattered in our interests and where we live, but we still want to know what's going on in each others' lives. Since I've been living here, it's been a bit harder, but we've been writing."

They finished the appetizer as they talked, and the plates were cleared. Betsy placed her hand out on the table, and Violet reached over to clasp it, a gentle smile playing across her face.

"How about you? Any siblings?"

"No, it was just me. I was spoiled by my parents and all the attention they gave me growing up."

Violet gazed around the restaurant. "Abritos's history is different from Earth's. We've been traveling in space for several centuries. My planet has had technology and scientific advancement since before yours had indoor plumbing."

As she spoke, Betsy nodded. She'd been alive for almost four hundred years. When she was born in a small village in Germany, the mere idea of America was not in anyone's thoughts. She knew everything Violet spoke of was true. "Is there a question in all that?"

"I guess I was wondering how strange, how *hard* it was for someone like you to grow up with all the changes that happened around you?" She leaned in, eyes focused on Betsy's.

"I started in Germany, or what we think of as Germany now. We tended to stay off the radar because of the magic and our connection to the aliens." Betsy leaned back, letting go of Violet's hand after squeezing it once the server came with their food. "On my one-hundredth birthday, Dad and Grandpa took Zuza and me to Torville Station Number Six. We spent several months—almost a year—studying the different aliens, and I learned to speak Galactic Standard. I'd studied it before but had never spoken it."

"Had you and Zuza been friends before that?"

"Not as much as afterward." Betsy took a bite of her panang curry and sighed. "When we returned, we decided to head to London. Zuza fell in love with the city, as did Grandpa. Dad and I decided to try out the 'New World.' It was the seventeen hundreds. Why not?"

"Have you lived here ever since?"

"No. I spent time in Africa. We established a training center there. Most of my time has been here, but I've tried to spend some time just about everywhere. But to get back to your original questions, there were times I lived in a cave. Times I lived in a castle, and over the years, I've seen just about everything. But when I was young, living in a hovel with a dirt floor, we had a panel on our wall that could create anything I asked for. The magic of technology has always been a part of my world, my home, my life, always. It has made experiencing the advancements a bit easier."

Violet laughed. "I hadn't thought about it that way, but I guess so. A kid from the Stone Age who spent half her time in a state-of-the-art space station with aliens. I guess shocking you wouldn't be that easy."

"Nope," Betsy said, smiling. "Not at all." Then she threw her bunched-up napkin at Violet. "Stone Age? Gah! I'm not *that* old, woman!"

Her eyes sparkled. "New question." Violet waved her fork, pointing it accusatorily at Betsy.

"Oh, no, what did I do?"

"For years, one of my favorite meals on space stations was sushi and tacos with vegemite."

Betsy locked her jaw shut, trying not to react, though her eyes widened. When she knew she could keep her voice level, she said, "Okay."

"Why can't I get that ... anywhere? Do you know how many places I've called? Everyone laughs. I had to special order vegemite from

Australia. Did you know there's a local grocery store here that sells it? Gods, I love the stuff. And I get the tacos and sushi from *two different restaurants!*" She waved two fingers in the air as if this were all Betsy's fault. "Two, not one. There's no one place that sells both."

"Okay, I'm still not following. You do know that Mexican and Japanese cuisine usually don't mix, right?"

"They do on the space stations. Tell me, why did your grandfather bring them to Torville Station Number Six together? Was he trying to bring us better food or punk us?"

That did it, Betsy laughed.

Land of Oz

Betsy

The ven zoomed around Betsy's room. They were getting bigger but would take the better part of the year to be as large as their mother, Beaver. She couldn't wait to see the mischief Wes got into as an adult ven. He was so smart now, but as an adult, he'd be unstoppable.

With a sigh, she pushed herself up. It was time to face the world. The last time she'd spoken to any of the magical people of Oz, the trio in that conference room, they hadn't seemed too keen on talking to her or anyone outside their bubble. Betsy didn't think today would be any better.

I wish I'd pushed for some way to contact them. I guess I could look up one of their places of business, but I'm not sure which would be the best. Are they really all magic practitioners? No, that must've been an act. There's no way.

She grunted and got ready. In the kitchen, she made coffee and had some yogurt. If she needed something more, she was sure the town would have some sort of restaurant.

It always annoyed her when she had coffee anywhere else. Her whole life, the panel had been making the best coffee just to her specifications. Being on Earth, it could pull beans from the top sources and be programmed to create exactly what she wanted. When she ended up drinking coffee anywhere else, no matter what words she threw at the baristas, the swill they served never turned out right.

Stop contemplating coffee, Betsy. You're procrastinating. It's just a town. No one there is going to attack you.

Just then, Wes landed on her head, and she yelped.

Ever since the chanzii had become refugees on Earth, the Ziner had been orbiting the planet. It was really nice when Betsy wanted to transport somewhere new. Horax and his crew were amazing at finding a safe place to set her, or anyone else, down. They'd find some position close to where she needed to be but away from prying eyes who may freak out at someone suddenly appearing.

Before Betsy had the qynad's help, she'd had to go through the steps of having the panel tap into one of the orbiting satellites and use the imagery to figure out where she could safely land. The Pillars had spots set up in their usual haunts, but Oz, Alabama, wasn't near anywhere they hung out.

Betsy squinted at the town. *That's not exactly true. It's close to where Dad and I lived when we first settled in America, Gods, two hundred years ago? Home sweet home. Okay, enough dawdling, time to go.*

She typed the last command, a location she wanted to transport, and her kitchen wavered and melted away. A moment later, Betsy materialized in a wooded area about a quarter-mile from town. Next to her stood a one-room schoolhouse she'd assumed was abandoned, but now, standing close to it, she realized it looked and felt used.

There was a path from the school to a sidewalk. She followed it and soon found herself in town. One of the first stores she passed sold gems. Gazing in the window, she saw Devlin. With a shrug, she walked in and headed for the counter.

His back was turned, but when he spun to face her, smile plastered and ready to do business, his whole demeanor shifted. "Oh. It's you. Pillar Doeth, correct? That's what you want us mere mortals to call you?" His face dropped and his voice shot cool daggers at her. "Why have you come to our town ... my store?"

"Good morning." His gruff attitude amused her, but it was what she had expected. She needed an "in," and he was her best bet. "If you'll permit me to call you Devlin, you can call me Betsy. I see no reason to be formal."

He grunted, and his shoulders dropped. "Fine, but my question stands. Why did you come to Oz?"

"I'd like to learn more about your town, the people here—who all are wizards—and more about your magic." She held up her hand. "I'm more than willing to share information."

"I was just going to say you'll need to speak with the mayor. She's probably down the road at the apothecary." He pointed in the direction he meant, but there was only one way to go from where she'd been. "You probably passed it on your way here. My shop is the last in town before the rural area, and I can't see you spending time out there."

"Thank you, and goodbye, Devlin." She bowed her head. "As always, it's been a pleasure."

Once on the street, Betsy took note of the different stores. Oz didn't have an online presence. The town was on the map, but none of the stores had websites. She took out her phone and snapped photos of the most idyllic small-town street she'd seen in years.

Shops of every type a person could want lined both sides. A bakery, a gem shop, and she bet, if she looked hard enough, a candlestick maker. The smells from Clean And Inspire made her want to get new soap and shampoo, but not today. She had a mission to finish, and it started at an apothecary.

A small bell rang as she opened the door. Amusement and a sense of inevitability overcame her when she saw Pearl Katz standing at the counter. Betsy had been so distracted by the town that she hadn't bothered to focus on store names. She saw the caduceus and walked right in.

She looked over her shoulder, and sure enough, 'Katz Apothecary' was emblazoned on the window.

Pearl's smile was wide and fake. "Why, Pillar Doeth. What brings you to Oz? Are you looking for a retirement home?"

She almost laughed at the barb. She liked Pearl and her sass. "I was hoping for an exchange of information. Someone told me I could find the mayor here. Would that be you?"

"No. That would be me." An older woman with strawberry-blond hair and blue eyes came from one of the aisles. "I'm Vicky Katz. My daughter named you one of the Pillars?"

"I am, but please, call me Betsy. I don't see any reason for formalities." Betsy held out a hand.

The other woman gazed at it for a moment with narrowed eyes before taking a long breath. "Fine. You can call me Vicky. I'm the mayor of this town. People look to me for guidance. I hope by speaking to you, I am not making a big mistake."

Betsy drew back her hand in quiet resignation. "I don't think you are, Vicky."

"Fine. Well, I need to get some work done here. Why doesn't Pearl take you back to our home? She can answer questions as well as I can."

"Mom, really? What about Dulaine?"

Vicky shot a hard look at her daughter. "I don't think Betsy will be a danger to your sister. Now, go home and send your dad here. He has some work to get done, and I'd like to have a family dinner tonight."

Pearl grumbled but came around the counter. "Fine. But just know, I'm telling Betsy everything. I won't hold back anything."

"Good," her mom said. "That will save us some time."

Pearl squawked and headed for the door. Betsy smiled and followed her. "This should be fun."

Vicky shrugged. "Pearl will run this town, if not the world, one day. I'm not sure what you did to get on her bad side. I didn't even know she had one before you, but don't worry, I'm sure you can get this all fixed."

Betsy wasn't as certain but followed the young woman anyway.

As they turned off the main road, a sense of recognition hit Betsy. Not the homes themselves, they were modern and she hadn't been to Oz, not since it had been named Oz, but there was a time she'd lived in this area. The twists and turns, the trees, the buzz in the air. Something touched deep within her, reminding her of years ago.

Did I walk this area with Dad before they named this town? Was close more than just near here, but here here?

They walked in silence as Betsy reconciled the past with the present. In short order, they arrived at a nice-looking Victorian house. "How old is your home?"

Pearl shrugged. "It's been restored to look like the original. I don't think it's from when the state was founded in the eighteen twenties, but it's close."

Wasn't there a house around here that sold the best sweet potato pies? Gods, was it this house? She swung her head around, trying to orient herself, but things had changed too much to be able to tell.

Inside, Pearl showed Betsy to a living room, then left to pour them each a sweet tea. Before she returned, a young girl, maybe nine or ten, came bounding into the room. Her brown hair flew around her head, but her gray eyes were sharp and intelligent. "Hi! I'm Dulaine. Who are you?"

"Why, hello there, Dulaine. I'm Betsy. How old are you?" There was something off about this girl, but Betsy couldn't pinpoint it. She figured, given some time, she'd suss it out.

"I'm eleven. I'll be twelve in a month and a half."

"Du-Drop, don't bother our guest," Pearl said, coming in carrying a tray with three glasses of tea. She placed it on the coffee table and then brought a glass to Betsy.

The tea was sweet, cool, and delicious. She hadn't had a good southern sweet tea in ages. "Thank you. This really hits the spot."

"I meant to ask, would you like a slice of pie? My family is known for it. A secret recipe that goes back several generations."

Betsy's brows rose. "It wouldn't happen to be sweet potato pie, would it?"

Eyebrows coming together in confusion, Pearl nodded slowly. "It is. How did you know?"

"As I mentioned before, I'm old. In a lifetime long, long ago, I lived near here with my dad. I don't know the exact location. Things have changed, but I have a memory of a pie. I know the chances are slim to none, but I've been dreaming of sweet potato pie. At this point, any made by a true southerner will probably do the trick." Betsy knew that wasn't strictly true. She really wanted the one from her past, but that, like many things, was a memory she could only visit with her eyes closed.

Betsy and the young girl looked at each other. "So, Dulaine, do you like to use fire?" Betsy loved it when her magic had first come out. And didn't Cassidy say everyone in town had magic? She had to have been exaggerating. Even on other planets where wizards were more common, full towns or villages were unheard of.

The young girl's shoulders dropped. "I'm broken. I am the only person in town who can't make fire ... or anything." Her slouched, sad demeanor nearly tore Betsy apart.

She wiped at her eyes and then saw Pearl standing at the entrance to the kitchen, a similarly sad expression on her face. Pearl straightened. "Nonsense, Du-Drop. You are perfect."

Betsy could only agree. But before she could say anything to this girl who didn't know her, Pearl handed Betsy a piece of pie. One bite, and she was transported to her past.

Once she'd eaten half the pie, she sighed. "Okay, so, you're telling me everyone in town can do magic? Cassidy wasn't exaggerating?"

Pearl's face hardened. "Why is that so hard to believe?"

"It's just ... that's not usually how it happens. And none of you age slowly. And you all have the same magic? Fire and imbuing?"

"Yes." She sounded exasperated. "You act as if there's so much more."

Betsy explained to Pearl and Dulaine about magic. A basic introduction about the elemental and non-elemental magics and how all wizards had one of each. If a magic user could master a third, they were considered an Elder.

"That last, which you say everyone in town has, is the rarest in the galaxy." Betsy shook her head.

"Rarest?" Pearl had made tea. She smiled, totally engaged in the lesson. "But that's what we all do, right? Applying magic to non-magical items?"

"Exactly. There is one alien race, the dwarves, who have the majority of the wizards who can imbue ... that was, until Oz. How many people are in this town?"

"The town has always been just under two hundred people." Pearl smiled. "We do bring in new people with marriage. Usually, they can't do magic, but Devlin's family has a way of finding people with potential."

"And always imbuing." Betsy shook her head.

"Of course. We teach it. I could teach you if you want."

The idea intrigued her. "I have time on Wednesday."

"But, Pearl, that's our day." Dulaine gazed up at her sister with wide eyes.

"It's one of them." Pearl bumped shoulders with her sister. "I'm not talking about the whole day, and you could be there too."

Betsy leaned forward, elbows on her knees. "I'm sorry for taking your day with your sister from you. Could I make it up by introducing you to one of our alien liaisons?"

Dulaine's eyes widened, and she turned to her sister. "Can I?"

Pearl sighed. "Which alien? One of the green ones?"

A smirk twitched the side of Betsy's face. "I was thinking one of the qynads ... the ones that look like dragons." A full smile blossomed as both sisters' mouths dropped open.

"Is it safe?"

"It is," Betsy assured Pearl. "But I'll need to give you translators, or you won't understand a word she says, and trust me when I tell you, Xantay has a lot to say."

"Okay," Pearl agreed. "Wednesday. But now, tell me, which non-elemental magic do you have, and what are the elemental magics?"

"I have life magic. I can work with plants and different spirit energies. Some with life magic are good with healing, and though I have healed, it isn't my specialty." Betsy gave Pearl a moment to process the information. "The elemental magic types are gas, liquid, solid, and energy. Fire is under the purview of energy. I have solid, so I can manipulate anything earth-related."

"Why do I feel there is more to your magic than just earth, Pillar Doeth?"

"Because, Ms. Katz, you are a very smart person." She sipped her tea. "There is a lot to learn about the full extent of magic, but we have time, and I'm willing to teach you."

From the floor where Dulaine sat drinking her tea, the girl danced. "A dragon. I'm going to meet a dragon."

18

Aliens, Everywhere I Turn!

Viera

The cafeteria of the Ziner wasn't the best place to read, but Viera wasn't having luck in the quiet of her and Thorn's apartment either, and she needed food. Her head pounded as she ate hot cereal and drank coffee.

The book Balzeno had given her explaining her bracelet and its usage was massive. The language in it, though English, was dense and just a bit awkward. She'd made it through the first chapter describing how the jewelry augmented her natural energy proficiency, and it finally made sense. The literal inch of reading had felt like a masters-level class in magic. There were additional inches for her other proficiencies.

The dwarf had added more than just what the bracelet did. It seemed the book knew what Viera needed to know and adapted ... if that was possible. The magical book made her head hurt worse. *Could I just ask a question, like with a magical grimoire, hold my hands out, and have the book open to the right page?* She huffed a laugh at her own thought.

She sipped her coffee, hoping the caffeine would strengthen the front-line defense in her head. Turning the page, the words in chapter two, covering how the beautiful bracelet interacted with time—*God, how much time have I spent reading this?*—started to blur.

A chime on the panel built into the table buzzed. Groaning, she tapped the receive button. "Ms. Kor, our lesson starts in two minutes. I expect you down in the training room, fed."

She tensed at Flower Prancer's voice. *Will I ever stop needing his training?*

"Hi, Ms. Kor!" Scout's exuberance as he skipped to the table, something she loved, even felt like sandpaper this morning.

"Hi, sweetie. How are you?"

"I'm great. Are you reading about the bracelet?"

"Yeah, but I need to get to training with the stubborn yonat."

The boy laughed. "Would you mind if I read some? The magic seems really interesting."

Viera snorted. "Have at it. Just be careful of the food and the book until you get back to the room."

"Sounds good." His smile was infectious. "I feel like a school r'grazz!"

About to stand to leave, Viera stopped. One of the ven, Fezzik, landed on her shoulder, his tawny fur tickling her ear. "A what now?"

"A r'grazz, you know, a bird. Hasn't that been in one of our lessons?"

One of Viera's eyebrows shot up. "Nope. And you feel like a bird because I'm letting you read my book?"

Scout laughed. "It's a saying. Acting like a r'grazz is acting foolish or flighty. Usually, it's in connection to flirting. Sometimes it's over something amazing, like this book, but it can be over anything."

"Ah, so you're a flitty bird over this huge book?"

"That I am, Ms. Kor."

Viera found herself chuckling and feeling lighter as she walked to meet Flower Prancer.

She entered the room with what she thought was many, many seconds to spare. "Ms. Kor! You're late!"

"No, I'm sure I have a few seconds."

"Check that pocket watch. You're two minutes late."

Her wristwatch told her she was ... *damn it all to hell.*

"Today, we're going to practice time bubbles and then sensing what is in them. Combining your abilities."

She nodded. The room was big enough for Viera to create a time bubble on the far side. Since Flower Prancer both had time as a proficiency and was an Elder, he easily walked into the area of stasis she'd created.

Once in, his tail switched, and the barrier turned opaque. A few moments later, he walked out. "Okay, Ms. Kor, keeping the barrier up, tell me how many stones are scattered within the time-space area you've created. Because of the way I set the pebbles, the number will change every two minutes."

Viera closed her eyes. The stones felt different in her time bubble than the rest of the air. It was as if Flower Prancer's magic left behind a bit of residue that felt scratchy to her senses. The problem was ... there weren't two or three stones but over a dozen.

Viera began to count, and the number shifted. The time it took to analyze and start counting had obviously taken more than the two minutes she'd been given.

"You're taking too long." His voice shot out, causing Viera to lose count.

Grumbling under her breath, she started over. Viera counted as quickly as she could. "Fourteen."

"No."

"Yes. I can feel it."

"That's, wait, yes, you took more than two minutes. That is the correct number."

She wanted to roll her eyes and smirk.

"You need to get this process faster. Let's do it again."

Viera dropped all her power as Flower Prancer collected his magical stones. As she created a new bubble, starting the process from the beginning, she contemplated her morning. First, the book, where she felt humbled by the dwarf from afar. Then Scout, the ven, and her mini language lesson. Now Flower Prancer and this.

How long until every part of my life isn't a lesson?

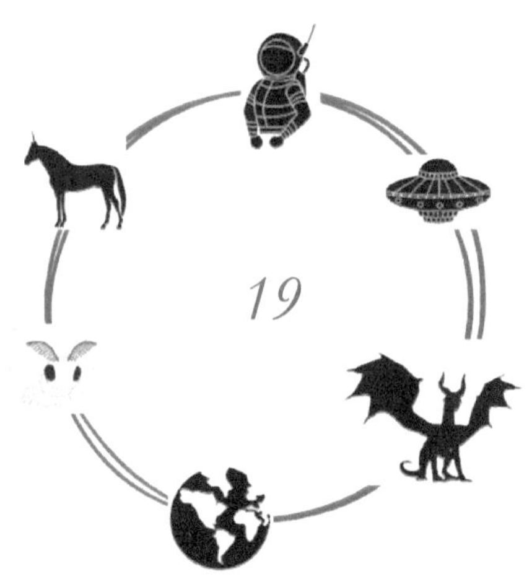

It's Not Always Paradise in the Tropics

Betsy

Why are there so many papers to sign to sell a house? Is there something in this stack that lets these people own my firstborn? More fool them!

When Viera decided to head off to Abritos and her mom begged Betsy to sell her house, Betsy forgot to take into consideration all the minutiae of the process. But the alternative was a stranger, who wouldn't have the family's best interest at heart, or Viera's family traveling, which they'd never loved to do.

"Only eight more pages for you to sign, Ms. Doeth, Mr. and Ms. Tobiath, then the house keys can be swapped, and the house is sold." The man in the suit smiled wide. Betsy had forgotten his name almost before he'd given it.

The muscles in Betsy's body turned to jelly as she signed her name again ... and again ... and again. The words on the pages had blurred into tiny ants of squiggles on the white sheets ages ago. Once she finished signing, the money would be sent to Viera's parents. Now that Viera worked as a liaison for the government, she didn't need to worry about money or housing in the unlikely event she ended up returning to Earth.

She flipped the paper, ready to sign, and found herself looking at the synthetic wood tabletop. A small sound of disbelief escaped her as she gazed at the fake wood, her hand hovering, waiting for the next line on which to sign. It took a few seconds for her mind to catch up to the idea she didn't need to sign any more papers.

She looked up, feeling dazed, and saw a similar look on the couple buying Viera's old house. The stack of papers had moved from the left side of him to the right side of her. They both smiled as if starting to realize the end was in sight.

"Excellent. That should cover everything. Now, Ms. Doeth, if you have the keys, I think we're done."

"I do." She closed her eyes and shook her head. "Sorry, for a few minutes, I wasn't sure the signing would ever end." She laughed, as did the couple, and reached into her purse to find the ring of keys. "This should be everything."

The man leading the meeting—Tom? Tad? Tim? Gah, something with a *T*—smiled. "And you did the walkthrough this morning? Everything checked out?"

The Tobiaths nodded. They looked as weary as Betsy felt. Mr. Tobiath sighed. "The house was exactly as we expected, John."

John? His name is John? Damn, I was way off.

"Well, then, it seems like we're done here."

Everyone stood and headed out toward their cars. Betsy wanted to get home. She thought a swim in the pool or playing with the ven would be amazing.

Maybe I'll call Violet. If she has this morning off. We could have some downtime together before checking on Xantay and how she's adjusting to island life.

After swimming a couple of laps in her pool, Betsy shifted to relaxing in the hot tub. She had about two hours before heading to the island to visit Xantay.

Betsy's home wasn't easy to find. The mailbox and structure for packages were available, but beyond that, anyone following the driveway would soon get confused and find themselves either changing their minds and turning around or taking an offshoot of the driveway that led back to the road and forgetting they hadn't visited at all. Few people knew the trick to getting to the house proper.

One way of reaching Betsy's home was having a code that a transporter would accept and arriving that way. That was how Violet arrived.

The air shimmered, and then she appeared in a bikini. Her skin was more a light aqua blue than some chanziians' turquoise skin. There was a spectrum that went from aqua to a dark teal green. Violet's hair, on the other hand, was such a dark purple it was almost black.

Betsy took a moment to catch her breath, gaping at how the suit perfectly covered the other woman's assets. It took her several seconds to realize she'd brought a bag ... probably with clothes to change into.

Violet turned. "This place is amazing. Your home. Did you do the decorating yourself?"

"I did. I wouldn't let just anyone out here."

A black meteor of fuzz descended from one of the trees and landed on Violet's shoulder. She startled, then laughed. "Wes, you scoundrel!" It didn't take long for Buttercup to follow, flying in slow circles above them. "They've gotten so big."

"If you don't get in here, you won't have time to unwind before we are needed on the island."

Her eyes narrowed. "Are we changing before heading out there? I just assumed we'd wear the suits and swim in the ocean."

Betsy leaned her head back and shut her eyes to think. She usually wore clothes to the island. "I guess that would save on time." When she looked back at Violet, she was in the hot tub across from her.

"Gods, this is amazing. It's heaven!" She sighed, then scooted around until her thigh touched Betsy's.

Betsy smiled. "I've been meaning to ask. Your hair"—she reached out to touch the silky strands—"is beautiful, by the way, but when you shift to look human, you're blond. Why such a big change? Don't you like your dark hair?"

A glow lit up Violet's face. "I do love my hair. Having hair this dark is rare on Abritos. Not even my siblings have anything this dark. But when I came here, I thought I'd try doing something completely different. Do you like the blond?"

"I do. It makes you look very sexy." She let her hand fall under the water to land on Violet's leg.

Violet leaned so their shoulders touched. They spent the next hour talking about their weekend. While Betsy was in Oz, Violet had a call with her family. There was a new niece in the fold.

Then they went inside to have lunch. Violet laughed over the process Americans went through to sell their homes. "How many papers?"

"A lot."

"But why? What were they all for?"

"You know? I'm not really sure. But I do fear for what all I may have signed away." Betsy winked. "If someone comes for Wes or Buttercup, it'll be their own damn fault."

Then, it was time to check in on Xantay. A quick scan let them know she was on the island.

It felt like a thousand mosquitos were biting into Betsy's skin as she landed on the island. The rain pelted down, and, clasping Violet's hand, she ran for the cover of the trees. Though the canopy didn't provide much, at least she didn't feel like she was being beaten up by the storm.

The two continued to run until they got to the protection of the structure. Once inside, the air conditioning, set way too low for their drenched condition, made Betsy feel like she was suddenly in a freezer.

Teeth clattering, she debated heading home for a sweatshirt and jeans. "Gods, why didn't I check the weather before coming here?"

Next to her, Violet nearly bent over in a burst of laughter. "I haven't made a mistake like this in years."

Betsy chuckled. "We were both too focused on swimming in the warm ocean water."

A peal of lightning and the crash of thunder made them both laugh harder.

Xantay came lumbering up the path behind them. "Why'd you two run? Swimming during a storm is the best." Her eyes glowed a deep blue. "You should've dove in and joined me."

The sound of Betsy's teeth clattering matched the shivers that ran down her body. "Too cold. I'm going to transport home, put on something warm, and be right back ... then we can talk." She didn't want to mention that even as big and red as Xantasy was, she hadn't seen anything in the storm.

"Would a fire help? I can set one in the pit under the awning." Xantay pointed out the door to an area protected from the rain.

Betsy and Violet agreed, and the qynad lightly blew to create the flame. Outside, near the pit, warmth infused Betsy as she sat on a log and sighed. Violet sat beside her as Xantay lumbered over to lie opposite them.

Once Betsy could feel her fingers, she said, "So, how are you enjoying Earth? The island? Your shuttle?"

"Oh! I love it all. I know I haven't really started doing anything as a liaison, but I'm really excited to meet more people and do things to represent the qynad. I know I can help show the Earthlings my people are intelligent and safe."

As few words as Horax had, his daughter was the opposite. Betsy marveled at how alike she was to most human teens. "What do you see as the biggest challenges you face?"

Her large head bobbed, a sign of her thinking and agitation. "I can't go and speak to a room of humans unless we spend time converting areas with language translators or convince all humans to wear earpieces."

"Gods," Betsy sighed. "Once the tech companies learn about adding the option into their specs, I can't imagine how much they'll charge."

"Why not flood the internet with freeware? That way, no one company will have access to how it's done." One of Violet's brows rose.

Xantay's body quivered. "It would be simple to do. Your planet's internet is so easy to manipulate. I could have the basic specs available in no time."

Betsy debated the pros and cons of the plan. "Overall, I like it. Let's wait until after the next press conference. I'd like a chance to tell people what's about to happen, so they know it's not malware. I want them to know it's a gift from the qynad so that everyone can speak with you. Then, maybe you can join us in a future speaking engagement."

"Oh!" Xantay perked up. "I'd love that. I can't wait to get out there and start bonding with some humans."

"I was hoping you'd say that." The chill started leaving Betsy's bones, though she still felt cold. As she shivered and spoke, Violet headed into the wickedly cold air-conditioned building. "Would you like to meet a young girl and her sister on Wednesday? She apparently doesn't have any magic in a town full of wizards. I'm trying to figure out how every person in this town could have magic while lifting her spirits."

"Do you think she'd be scared of me?" The red qynad sounded pensive and a bit sad.

A wide smile spread on Betsy's face. "Not once she gets to know you."

Violet came out carrying a bunch of stuff. "I had the panel create two sweatshirts, marshmallows, chocolate bars, and graham crackers. As long as a tropical island is making us feel chilled to the bone, we may as well play up the campfire."

Betsy slipped on the warm top, and the two roasted the sugary delights on long forks. For a moment, Xantay gazed at the extended flatware but then shrugged. "I'm going back out to the ocean, better appetizers there. When you're done, let me know. We can have a proper dinner together."

Dessert before dinner. Betsy couldn't imagine a better meal.

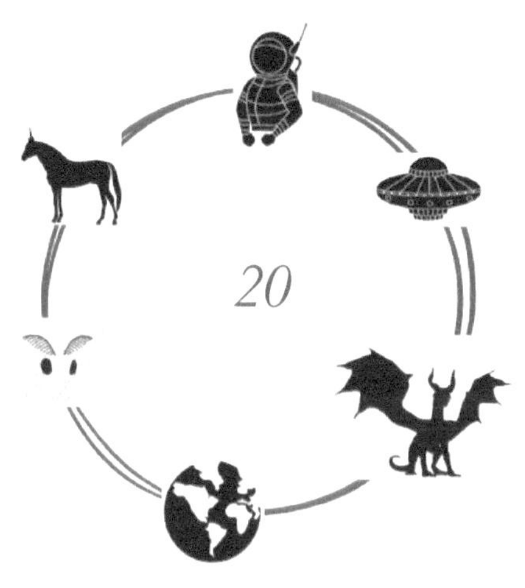

I Am The Boss of You

Betsy

During dinner—steak and potatoes with salad and wine—Betsy, Violet, and Xantay traded stories of their adventures in the different space stations. Some of Xantay's adventures with Horax and her siblings were so funny, they had them laughing hard enough that none of them noticed when the rain stopped.

As warm as it was on the island, the group decided on an evening swim.

It was nice to get out and play with the qynad. Xantay liked to dive, then shoot up into the air, spinning vertically, letting the ocean water spray off her in all directions before twisting and diving back into the sea. She did her acrobatics far enough out that the waves didn't threaten to capsize Betsy or Violet, but they did laugh a lot the whole time watching her.

After an hour or so, the two women returned to the beach. The sun had dipped below the horizon, and the sky deepened to a dark purple, almost black. A few adventurous stars started twinkling.

Betsy couldn't hold back a yawn. "I'm sorry. The house sale started at seven-thirty this morning. And we have to be in New York to meet with Juk at nine, his time, *tomorrow* morning. I have no idea how or when my schedule got so busy."

Violet wrapped an arm around her waist. "We could each head home. There's no reason to prolong the evening. I'm really enjoying myself, but it's late."

"Or"—Betsy copied Violet's action and slid her arm around the other woman and squeezed her close, liking how well they fit together—"you could spend the night at my place. Then I wouldn't have to drive over in the morning. I mean, it would only be practical, right?" When Violet got quiet, something in Betsy hurt, but she understood. She'd taken their flirtations a step too far. "You know I have a lot of guest rooms. I mean ... you wouldn't have to ... um." *Gods above, I sound like a teenage fool!* She slowly let her arm fall, ready to step away.

It was easy to forget how strong the chanzii were, especially the petite ones. As a race, they were stronger than humans, even the ones who looked frail and in need of protection. Violet held Betsy tight. "Slow down, Earthling. You need to breathe. It's late, and we're both tired. I like the idea of spending the night ... and *not* in a guest room. I just also need sleep. Could we do that?"

An emotion Betsy didn't understand filled her. She realized she was smiling like a goof as she stared into the woods ahead of them, and it dawned on her that she couldn't imagine anything that sounded better right then. She was so tired from the day she'd had, but the feeling of Violet beside her felt so right.

"Betsy? Did you hear me? Did I break you?"

She chuckled. "No, I mean yes, and not quite. And yes, having you spend the night *sleeping* over sounds just about perfect."

The two said their goodbyes to Xantay and transported back to Wisconsin. The ven zoomed around them, excited to have their staff back, especially when they saw two sets of hands to give them scratches and pets.

It didn't take long to change for bed. Betsy lent Violet a tank top and shorts pajama set, and the two settled in. Violet leaned over for a kiss. "Goodnight, Betsy. I'm really glad we're doing this." She rolled over to her side.

Betsy curled in, wrapping her arm around Violet. They fit together perfectly. "Me too." She was asleep almost before her eyes shut.

Betsy stretched out the next morning, the sun lighting the room in warm shades. After a yawn, she opened her eyes and saw Violet on her side, gazing back at her. "Gods, you are beautiful."

Violet traced Betsy's face from the tip of her forehead to her chin. "I agree, lovely." She leaned forward and brushed her mouth against Betsy's.

Before she could move away, Betsy raked her fingers through Violet's dark-purple locks, marveling at how the sun almost made them darker, and pulled her in for a deeper kiss. Ever since they'd begun flirting, all she'd wanted to do was taste this woman, this alien, this masterpiece of elegance and perfection, everywhere she could.

Her other hand slid up Violet's side, under the tank top, and tugged until she lay on top of Betsy, their legs intertwined. Enjoying the silky sensation, Betsy slowly glided her hand up until her thumb caressed the other woman's breast.

Violet moaned in her mouth, rubbing and gyrating above her. She began trailing kisses across Betsy's cheek toward her ear, where she bit down. Tiny spikes of pain and pleasure radiated to Betsy's core. Then Violet sat back and slipped off her top. Her perfect breasts, a bit larger than could fit in Betsy's hands, bounced free from the fabric. "Off with your clothes, Pillar Doeth."

"As you wish, Major North." Violet didn't stop straddling Betsy, so stripping involved a lot of wiggling and rubbing of body parts. By the time she was done, her breathing came fast and rough.

Desire overcoming her, Betsy reached up and stroked the perfect globes above her. She wanted to drag them down for a lick, but the smirk on Violet's mouth told her she wasn't getting her way so easily.

"I want your hands behind your head, Pillar, and keep them there. If you don't behave—"

"Do I get to have my way with you when we're done, Major North?" She raised one brow in defiance but put her hands where commanded.

"We'll see." In a smooth move, Violet leaned down and gently scraped her teeth over Betsy's nipple, then sucked. She scooted lower, letting her other hand slowly rub its way down Betsy's abs to her hip.

With a groan, Betsy bucked, trying to guide Violet's hand. She only stroked her thumb near the junction of the leg in circles that got bigger and bigger. Her attention to Betsy's breast got more intense, sucking and nibbling.

Heat grew within her, and she felt herself getting wet. It wouldn't take much more.

With a strong suck, Violet moved to the other breast and her finger gently traced a path up through her slickness to her clit. "Gods, you are wet."

Betsy whimpered.

"Do you want more of this?" Violet lightly played with her center. Then her mouth came down. The heat and pressure caused Betsy to arch up, desperate for the other woman.

"Gods, yes!" Betsy's voice was barely a breath.

One hand went to her lower belly, holding her down. With the other, Violet pressed fingers into her, finding a rhythm. The hand on her stomach moved up to her nipple and began to explore.

Betsy's universe fractured. She yelled out her desire as Violet played her body expertly. It had been so long. Her mind and soul rode the orgasm Violet gave. When the waves of mind-numbing pleasure finished radiating through her body, Violet curled into her, a satisfied smile on her face. "That was fun."

"My turn." Betsy wished she sounded more dominant, but after what Violet had done to her, every muscle in her body felt like putty.

"Do we have time? Because our meeting starts soon. I figure this gives us both something to look forward to."

With a moan, Betsy looked at the clock, then pulled Violet in for a kiss. "Shower, meeting, then more sexy time."

"Absolutely not. There is no way that can happen." Juk's face scrunched up, though his nostrils flared. "I forbid it."

Leaning back in her seat, Betsy considered the young man. With a slight push of magic, she planted the thought: *I really want to study all the files on the Pillars. Once and for all, I'll learn that I am not the boss around here.* She'd been patient with him, but it was time.

Like a slow-motion claymation movie, his face fell until his mouth hung open slightly, then he shook his head. Then his eyes narrowed. "I mean it, Bets ... er, Pillar Doeth, no."

"I think it's really cute that you believe I'm asking and not informing you, Juk. Despite what's happening in your head, here are the facts. I really think you should go back to the files you *told* me you read and study them ... *all* of them. Read them back to the initial ones, not just the last few years." She took a steadying breath and sipped her coffee.

Once again, Miranda had brought her coffee and a pastry. This time, it was donut holes, which were often dry, but these were amazing. She shared them with Violet, who'd also been handed a coffee.

For good measure, Betsy sampled a cherry donut hole before continuing. "Juk, you are not my boss. Not only that, you have no say in what I do." His face started to get red, but she held up a hand forestalling any comments. "This will shock you, but Mr. Mard is also not my boss." She sipped her drink to let that sink in. "I created this department just after the Civil War. The United States was starting to figure things out ... it was still pretty behind, but it was getting there. My grandpa was against it, but he mostly lived in London, very interesting people living there at the time. So, my dad and I decided to create a place where a select few humans would know about aliens. It was eventually done on all planets."

"But ... you? This is your department?" Juk sputtered.

"It is."

"But you don't even have an office." He smirked. "Anyone of importance has an office."

His expression told her he thought he'd won his argument. Betsy wasn't sure if they specifically hired unintelligent people or if they selected the lowest of the low to continually punish her for being the female founder of such a prestigious department.

"Okay, Juk, this is what we're going to do. First of all, I'm going to bring Xantay to meet Dulaine Wednesday. I promised the girl—not to mention Xantay—and it *will* happen." Betsy took a breath, realizing she was getting snarky. "It's really none of your business. I only told you so you'd be aware, nothing more."

"I want it on record that I refused this request." His voice sounded snappish.

"No request. Please get it through that thick skull of yours." She sighed. "I may have to speak with Orson about a new contact person. He thought you'd be teachable ... I'm not seeing that as possible. Every one of these meetings results in you being impertinent, disrespectful, and ignorant. One or two of these are manageable, but all three? Gods above, you're onerous."

His mouth pursed together, but he didn't say anything. She nodded once. "What I need you to do is contact Xantay and work with her so our press conference next week can include her."

"The one in Dubai?" His face remained tight, and his words were flat.

She could strangle him. If she used magic, there'd be no way to trace it back to her. "Juk, you've never sent me the itinerary of places you've arranged. You tell me the current week's location, and that's it. So, if you've scheduled Dubai for next week, then yes, that's what I want."

One side of his mouth quirked up. "You do know there's a website ... the one you discuss during your talks. It has a full schedule linked. Would you like me to help you navigate to the—"

His chair disintegrated beneath him, and she heard his head hit the ground as he fell. "If that is all, Youngling, then we shall leave. You *do* know how to contact Xantay, right? Or do you need one of us to explain it to you?"

His eyes were wide, and his mouth hung open as Betsy and Violet walked out of the conference room. In the lobby, Betsy made a beeline to Miranda's desk. "There's a bit of a mess in there.

You'll need to call someone from janitorial. Also, a new chair will be needed."

Miranda's eyes widened, but she merely nodded.

Violet smiled wide. "Do you have an office in this building?"

"Yes, ma'am," Miranda said before Betsy could answer. "The full top floor belongs to Pillar Doeth. The executive suit. It has a panoramic view of Manhattan and an apartment in case she ever wants to spend the night in our fair city."

Behind her, she heard Juk gasp. "You ... wait, that's *your* office? I always thought it was Mr. Mard's or some other executive."

Betsy paused, debating ignoring him. Then Miranda spoke. "It does belong to an executive, dear, our top executive. Bless your heart for not knowing. It's rather precious of you." Her smile was so sweet that Betsy thought she may need to check for cavities.

"Then why don't you ever use it?" His voice was sharp.

Violet bumped shoulders with her. "Yeah, I'm kind of curious about that too."

Betsy shrugged. "I used to when I lived in New York, but I like the speed and energy of Madison better. Once the chanzii refugees got here, it was easier to be close at hand, and my regular time in the office just sort of"—she shrugged—"I don't know. It didn't seem as important."

"Do you see yourself using the offices here again in the future?" Violet twined her fingers with Betsy's.

"Maybe. It's a great office." She looked intently at Violet. "It would be perfect for two people to work out of."

A mischievous glint sparkled in Violet's eyes.

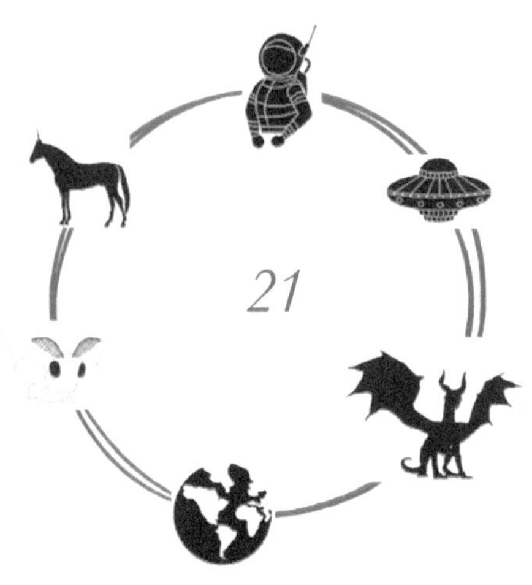

A New Friend

Dulaine

Dulaine's jaw hurt from how tight she clenched it. It wasn't that Kirke wasn't nice ... well, she wasn't, but she also wasn't mean. It was just that she never listened to what she had to say.

"Again, Dulaine, reach down to the pit of your belly and feel the warmth. Imagine the candle on the corner of the table with a nice dancing flame on its wick, then push that image out." It felt like Kirke wanted to see into Dulaine's brain. "Do you think you can do it ... this time?"

With some effort, Dulaine relaxed her jaw. Her head hurt from the tension she held in her body. She breathed in slowly through her nose, just like Pearl taught her, then let it out quickly through her mouth, letting her cheeks puff out. Her sister hadn't taught her that. It just amused her.

Kirke had told her the same steps every day for years. Sometimes, over and over. It was like she thought her a fool. Well, there were times, they did regular school things, like math and history. She liked those days better. The magic lessons were awful. Kirke made Dulaine feel like an idiot.

"I'll do my best." It was all she could promise. She knew she couldn't do it. When she reached into her belly, she didn't feel heat or anything burning. She only felt a cool, relaxing ocean of calm. It was how she didn't get angry at being told the same thing over and over. It was why being a magical dud in a town of the most amazing people on the planet didn't make her head explode. She knew, on really stressful days, she could go home and take a relaxing bath. The water always soothed her.

She closed her eyes and found her center. It felt like she swam in her own void, cool and relaxed. Once, she added the image of a candlestick with a flame, just like she'd been told, but it didn't seem to fit. Despite that, she tried again and again. Once she forced the image, she tried pushing it out.

Nothing.

Again.

As always.

Her mind wavered between annoyed and numb. It was hard to be upset about something she knew couldn't change.

A knock came at the door. Both Dulaine and Kirke looked at who would actually knock. Dulaine recognized Betsy. Kirke's face tightened. "Who are you?"

"It's Betsy! She promised to bring me a friend to meet. Did you? Is she here?"

Pearl came in from behind the wizard. That was what Betsy called herself: a wizard. It was such a cool name.

That's what I want to be, a wizard. Forget lighting a candle. I want to be like Betsy. I wonder if that's possible. What did she say she could do?

"Hi, Kirke, this is Pillar Doeth. She came to get a tour of the town and to let Dulaine meet one of the aliens. I understand it's a school day, but this was the best time all around."

"Pearl, I recognize you think you know what's best for your sister, but she's eleven and needs to be in school."

A sense of dread filled Dulaine. *Will Kirke ruin this for me? What if I don't get to meet the qynad? This is a dream for me.*

"An hour or so will not ruin my sister's future prospects. I have it on good authority that she is ahead in all her studies." Pearl's face stiffened as if she were ready to fight.

"And your parents? Miss Katz? What does the mayor think of this intrusion on her daughter's education?"

Dulaine shrunk from the fight. She saw Pearl's face shift from anger to annoyance. The other woman, Betsy, didn't give away any of her emotions. *I want to be like that. A totally unreadable statue. I wonder if she'd teach me her trick if I ask nicely. She should teach Pearl too. I can tell all of my sister's emotions. It's like reading a book.*

"I'm going to take Dulaine now. We'll be back in an hour and a half. She'll spend the first part of the time with Xantay while I show Pillar Doeth around town. Then my sister will have lunch and return for afternoon lessons. I doubt she'll fall too far behind, Kirke." Her tone spoke volumes, and Dulaine didn't wait for any other discussion. She stood and followed.

In the field was a huge red dragon ... qynad. Dulaine's heart beat fast in her chest and she wasn't sure she could breathe. Betsy went up to the dragon. "Xantay, this is Dulaine. She's very eager to meet you."

A series of snarls and roars emanated from the dragon's mouth, and Dulaine trembled. She wanted to be brave, to walk up to the fierce beast, and ... *did qynads shake hand to wing? How did one properly greet a dragon ... er, qynad?*

Betsy leaned in toward the qynad, then glanced over her shoulder at Dulaine. "Oh, hell." She spun and jogged back to Dulaine, dropping to her knees. "I'm so sorry. I don't know how I forgot. Here, put this in your ear." She handed Dulaine something that looked like the Bluetooth device Dulaine saw people using in magazine ads.

It took a moment to get it situated correctly, but once she did, the red beast said in an excited tone, "Hi, I'm Xantay, and I'm really happy to spend some time with you, tiny human. Would you like to sit and talk with me?"

Dulaine's jaw dropped open. "She speaks English?"

"No." Betsy's smile was huge. "That earpiece translates any alien language so you can understand them. Now, Pearl is going to give me a full tour of the main street of town. Why don't you spend some time with Xantay. You're her first Earthling, besides me and the other Pillars."

Heart beating fast, Dulaine wanted to be brave. As she walked over to the qynad, she saw Pearl and Betsy watching. She knew they had things to do, so she waved them off.

Glancing over Xantay, she noted that the tips of her wings were black. "Oh! You're not all red, are you?"

"Oh, no. Very few of us are fully one color." She lifted a wing and shimmied left and right. "My mom was a red dragon. She was huge and fierce. Dad is smaller and blue. I got my coloring from Mom. I wouldn't have minded being a blue dragon, but I love the color red. How about you? Did you get your … um … coloring? From your parents?"

Dulaine laughed. "I have the same brown hair as my dad." She fluffed the end of her wavy hair with the tips of her fingers. "But no one has gray eyes like me. Dad's eyes are brown and Mom's are blue. I don't mind mine, though."

They sat looking at each other for a few seconds, then Xantay quivered as if excited. "Okay, you are my test run with humans. That's what Betsy, er Pillar Doeth, told me. I need to practice speaking with other races. Do you have any questions about the qynads?"

There were so many questions that Dulaine didn't know where to start. After taking another calming breath, she nodded. "I have a lot of them. Like, do you have magic, like Betsy? Are you a wizard?"

"Me? No. There aren't many qynads who are also wizards. Those of us who are tend to have sensing magic as the non-elemental, though a few qynads have life. I've never heard of any qynads with time or imbuing as their proficiency. As for the elemental magic, it's mostly solid, which is great for building elaborate cave systems for our hoards."

"Oh, my God, qynads really do have hoards? What do you hoard, coins? Gold? Books?"

Xantay's eyes widened a bit. "Oh, no, not that. Qynads live in groups, like several families together. All the kids are brought up together."

"Like our town?"

"Not quite." Xantay gazed up at the sky. "For me, I could go to any of the adults to get help. Though I knew who my parents were, it really didn't matter. Any kid could go to any adult if they had a problem, needed an answer, or were hurt. We call each of these family communities a hoard."

"Oh! It sounds like a hippie commune." Dulaine smiled. "I studied those in history class."

"Hippie commune. I may have to look that up and see. It would make describing our hoards much easier."

Dulaine sat in the grass, leaning back on her hands. "So, no hoards like the legends of dragons here on Earth, huh?"

"Well, I mean, I do love spoons. We don't have them back home. They're so interesting. My collection is rather impressive. My dad likes those decorative pillows humanoids put on couches ... oh, no!" The qynad shut her maw with an audible snap. "Please don't tell anyone I said anything about this."

Dulaine's mouth dropped open and her eyes widened. "Are you saying you have a hoard of spoons hidden away?"

"It's a secret I'm not supposed to tell. If that gets out and they trace it back to me, I'll never be a liaison."

"I promise. But ... do all qynads collect spoons? Or pillows? Or something?"

"Oh, um, yes. We all like something different. At first, my dad collected bean bags, but apparently, one claw snagged a giant pink one he'd been using as a bed"—she held up one of her sharp digits—"and clean-up was a bear!"

"Oh, gosh!" Dulaine shook her head. The idea of everything she heard almost overwhelmed her. Then a laugh bubbled out as she pictured a large blue qynad situating himself on a pink beanbag and the thing exploding everywhere. "So you're saying every qynad has a different thing they like to collect?"

"And it's a huge secret."

"Don't worry," Dulaine assured her. "I'm very good with secrets."

215

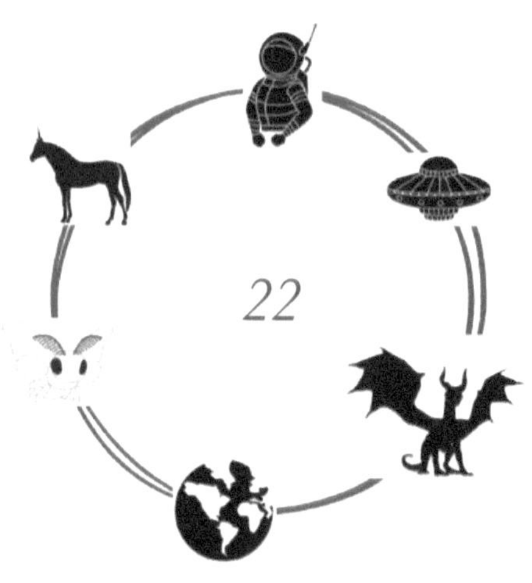

Out and About

Betsy

Betsy wasn't sure what it was about Dulaine, but she felt there was more to the girl than a magical dud in a town of magical wonders. She hoped an hour with Xantay would help bring her out of her shell and give her something to remember.

For now, she knew she had to focus on Pearl and Oz. "So, you said you just received a medical degree. Is there a medical facility in town? Does your population avoid major hospitals for a reason?"

Of all the responses Betsy expected, a laugh wasn't high on the list. "People in Oz usually don't need doctors."

"Really? Then why the degree? And why in four years?"

"I would think the four years would be obvious." Pearl sounded disappointed. "I have a huge secret to keep, not to mention we magic users can't use technology."

An earlier conversation with the Pillars came back to Betsy. Hadn't Zuza said something about this? People who didn't own the magic but instead used the magic around them? "Do you mean you can't or don't?"

Pearl bristled. "Well, I can, but it's hard. I have to ensure I don't tap into any of my magic. But why are you asking this? You use magic. You know this." Her voice was laced with derision.

Great, we're back to the Pearl of day one. Just what we needed.

With slow motions, Betsy reached into her pocket and pulled out her cell phone. "I use this daily, as do all the Pillars. I'm starting to form some theories, Pearl, but if you could control your use of magic for a few seconds, I'd like to turn this off before its circuits fry."

Pearl's eyes widened. "You use a cell phone? Like regularly?"

"I do. I also use computers and other state-of-the-art technology. Even while using my magic. I suddenly understand why none of your town is online."

They'd reached the edge of Oz and Devlin's gem shop. Pearl headed for the door. "I don't know what to say about this." Once inside, her voice rose. "Devlin! We need to talk."

"Well, good day to you too, Pearl. How are you this fine Wednesday?" His low, soothing voice blanketed the store. As before, he stood behind the counter, working. After he looked up, he sighed, and his voice became exasperated. "Ah, Pillar Doeth, welcome to my store."

With a grunt, Pearl waved her hand. "Enough of that. She brought a dragon—"

"A qynad."

"Oh, right, a qynad to meet Dulaine. My sister is happier than I've seen her in a long time. We're giving the wizard an hour of our best behavior."

The storekeeper froze, eyes widening. "There's a dragon in town?"

"Qynad," Betsy repeated. She began to think she should keep track of how many times she ended up saying the word.

"Yes, Devlin, keep up. I'm taking Betsy on a tour, letting her learn about our town. Did you know she has a cell phone and can use it and a computer while using her magic?"

His jaw dropped. "Say what? But that's not possible."

She sighed. The rest of her morning passed in front of her eyes in a flash. "There are two ways to access magic. The majority of people have magic within themselves. We are wizards. A very small subset of people can tap into the magic around them, pulling it in and utilizing it. It is an almost unheard-of subset of magic users. We'll call you witches. As it goes, it appears that's what the people of your town are. Because you create an energy field when you manipulate the magic around yourselves versus what we do when using the magic within, it messes with the tech."

The two gaped at her. Then Pearl's eyes narrowed. "Is there a way to shift how we use magic? Can we become ... wizards?"

Betsy shrugged. "I'll have to do some research before I answer that question. It's a bigger idea than just changing your relationship with your power."

"Good God, we're going to have to have a town meeting. Pearl, you'll need to talk with your mom about this." There was wonder in his voice. Betsy thought if she had a book or ten, he'd volunteer to do the research for her.

"I know." Pearl, on the other hand, was all business.

Devlin ducked down and a shuffling sound could be heard. Then he came back up with a pair of green jade stones. He placed the stones on the counter, then shook his head. "No, this isn't right. You can use a cell phone. Darn." He disappeared again. After a few seconds, he popped up like a weird game of whack-a-mole. Betsy wondered if he would drop down again. This time, he had a large piece of onyx. "Okay, this is something I've imbued. I'd like to thank you for the information you've given by offering Dulaine time with a dragon."

Betsy sighed. She wasn't sure if he'd ever learn the right name.

"What does this stone do?"

"If you activate it, it will amplify your voice like a microphone. This is the type of thing we use in town because we don't have technology."

"Thank you. I appreciate the gift." She tapped the jade stones. "What were these?"

"Oh, it's silly if you can use a cell phone. We all carry them. They're our communication stones. Everyone who has one can connect with each other ... if you focus on them and push a bit of your magic ... your will into contacting them." One of his shoulders bounced up in a small shrug. "I've made them for a group so you can state who you want to contact."

Shutting her eyes, Betsy thought about the stones. "How far of a range do they get?"

"I don't know. I've never tested that. But any distance we've tried, they've worked." The twinkle in his eyes let her know he liked the idea of the challenge.

"If you don't mind, I'll take the jade stones. I'd like to see if they work off-planet. I'm not always on Earth. Nor are the people I need to speak with."

His eyes widened in understanding as he shifted to look toward the field where an alien was playing with Dulaine. "Why not take both? It would be an honor, especially if you could bring me back data on my magic."

"With pleasure." She was about to turn, then hesitated. "If you're thinking of heading out to meet the qynad, take this." Betsy reached into her bag and pulled out another earpiece translator. "It translates any alien speech to your language. I have it calibrated to Earth American English." She thought for a moment. "The technology is surprisingly simple. I don't think your magic will do too much to mess it up."

His eyes narrowed. "You wouldn't happen to have two of those, would you?"

Betsy wondered if he had a partner or worried about the first shorting out and shrugged. "Sure." She handed him another one. She had a few more, but not enough for everyone in town. Violet had been right. They needed to stock up.

The next stop was the town's bakery. The woman running the shop, Maleah, was as sweet as the items she produced. Betsy felt like she had walked into her grandma's kitchen ... if she'd ever had a grandma's kitchen to walk into.

"Why, Pearl, you brought a friend. Do you both want a slice of flourless chocolate cake? It's the special this week, as you know."

"Yes and make them to-go. Maleah, this is Betsy, one of the five magic wizards working with the government and aliens all these years."

The woman, who felt older than Betsy but looked to be maybe in her forties, gave her a warm smile. "It sounds like you do a lot of additional work. Take this brownie for when you need some extra motivation." She winked. "Just don't gobble it up willy-nilly like a youngster, you hear."

Betsy laughed. She wanted to bottle this woman up and take her with her wherever she went.

Shenel ran the next store, Clean And Inspire. She acted like a person's favorite aunt. Like Devlin, she had a lot of questions about magic and how Betsy's differed from that of the town. She also kept referring to Xantay as a dragon.

Why is figuring out the word qynad so hard? Should I make cards with the proper name?

As they left, she gave Betsy a free sample basket. The soaps were labeled Liveliness Lather. "Use this in the morning to help you feel refreshed, even when sleep isn't as readily available as you may like."

She tried to force a smile. "Thank you."

Betsy waited until they were outside to shake her head. Every soap and lotion company in the world touted how invigorating their products were. It got to be as obnoxious as every other commercial out there.

Cassidy squealed when they walked into the next store. That was until she saw Betsy. "Oh, it's you. The oldest woman on Earth." She rolled her eyes. "Great." Then she flounced back behind the counter.

"Actually, Ania in Australia is about a hundred and fifty years older than me, and Zuza in London is about a hundred years older, though he's male not female. But I do come in third. But that's only on Earth. By galactic standards, there are plenty older than me." Her tone was flat, and at the end, she shrugged.

"Whatever." She scrunched up her mouth, then huffed. "Dad, Pop, we have a customer."

"Can you handle it?"

"No."

Two men came out from the back. They looked very similar. Both were about six feet tall with salt and pepper hair. They had brown eyes and a face full of smile lines. Though they looked fit, they were each a bit hefty and looked like the types who were always happy. The only difference she saw was that one had a beard and mustache, and the other didn't.

After a moment of silence where Pearl and Cassidy stared at each other, having a silent conversation—though Betsy was pretty sure it was just that they were close friends—Pearl stepped forward. "Betsy, this is Trent and Jesse, Cassidy's parents. They run the paper shop. Trent, Jesse, this is Betsy, she's—"

"She's the wizard who tried to arrest us in New York," Cassidy spat out.

It took everything in Betsy to not react or respond. The men smiled as if they'd expected nothing less from their daughter.

Pearl sighed. "She didn't. She pulled us into a private room to speak with us so that others, including those with cameras, wouldn't figure out our identities. Anyway, she's in town getting a tour."

After Pearl explained everything, Trent—or was it Jesse? No one had specified which was which—offered Betsy a sheet of paper that would turn a spell gone wrong into flowers with a bit of intent and a small tear. The sheet held three iterations of the spell.

Betsy was intrigued by the magic and thrilled to get this imbued item. "Thank you. This is amazing."

Cassidy smirked. "You know, we also sell incense. If you're interested, you should try this." She tossed a package at Betsy.

One of her parents, the one with the beard, shook his head. "Is that a good idea?"

"Why not? It's to enhance memories. I'm sure someone as worldly as a Pillar could only get good things from past memories." The challenge in the teen's eyes amused Betsy more than anything. She added the incense to her pile.

Pearl led Betsy to the end of the block, pointing out several other hot spots, but the only other shop they went into was her parents' apothecary. The conversation went similarly to the others, save one part.

"You left my eleven-year-old with a dragon?"

"A qynad."

"A beast who could eat her in one bite?"

"A qynad, Mayor Katz, and why would Xantay do such a thing? She's a liaison for her planet. She's here to impress, not dine." Betsy couldn't believe the ignorance of these people.

"But a dragon? With my daughter?"

"Qynad, ma'am."

"I can't believe you thought introducing my young child to an alien without my permission was acceptable."

Pearl huffed an annoyed sound. "I set this up, Mom. She didn't just up and decide to do this on her own."

"When can I meet this dragon?"

"Qynad." *What is my count?*

"I have meetings today and tomorrow. Saturday. Bring the alien back Saturday."

Betsy rubbed her face. "Is that a request or a demand?"

"I am Dulaine's mother. I deserve to have time to speak at length with this dragon. It's a matter of safety. As for now, please remove my daughter from this dangerous situation."

The hour was well over, and Betsy was ready to head home, so this demand, though rude, was fine by her. "As you wish."

Mr. Katz ran out from the back. "Dear, we can't be the only store that doesn't gift Pillar Doeth before she leaves. I have prepared this for her."

Vicky Katz huffed and turned. "Whatever." She walked toward the back. "I'll see you Saturday."

"Mr. Katz."

"Please, call me Porter. And here is a tincture. It accelerates the healing of just about any wound, as long as the limb is still available."

One of Betsy's brows rose. "Any wound? Even old ones?"

"Oh, sure. As long as the bits are there to be healed."

She bowed her head. "Thank you."

After that, Betsy walked back to the school with Pearl. They found Dulaine and Xantay playing chess and talking up a storm. Pearl collected her sister. "It's time to eat."

Both seemed saddened by the end of their play date.

Betsy shook her head but spoke loud enough for Dulaine to hear. "Xantay, Dulaine's parents have requested another appointment on Saturday. They'd like a personal visit to ascertain the safety of their youngest spending time with a qynad. If you'll okay the day, I'll make the arrangement."

Xantay's eyes sparkled, but she took a moment. "I believe I can clear my schedule, Pillar Doeth."

Behind her, Dulaine cheered.

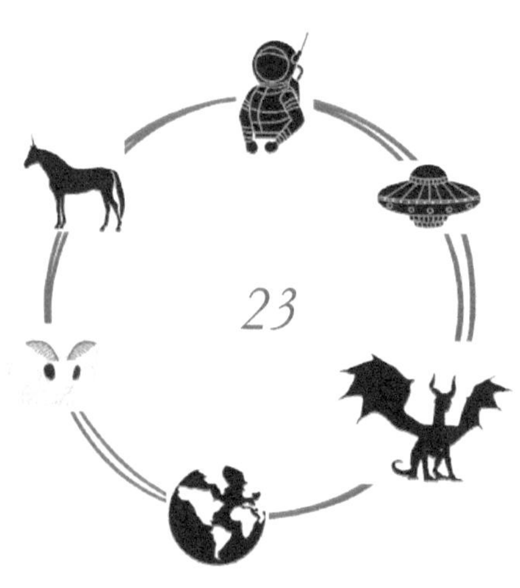

23

Shrimp on the Barbie

Betsy

As Betsy watched the latest cooking competition on television, she debated if she wanted to try to bake any of the sweet treats the contestants were making. She wasn't sure she could, but even a failed attempt would probably taste good.

Her phone rang and she answered it after checking the display. "Hi, Violet. Would you ever want to try a white chocolate sponge cake with blackberry mousse, or a strawberry and coconut roll cake or ... wait, um, a huckleberry and lemon poppy seed cake with hazelnut buttercream?"

"Are you watching a cooking competition? Because those all sound delicious but also a bit suspicious."

Betsy laughed. "Guilty. But that doesn't answer my question."

"I'd like to try them all and judge which one I like best. Can you do that?"

"Gods, are you trying to kill me? I'm not that good of a baker." She groaned.

"What if I came over and helped you?" There was a wicked edge to Violet's voice.

Betsy leaned back on her couch, a warmth suffusing her. "Do you know how to bake?"

"Nope, but that would be half the fun, right?" Violet laughed.

The tension from her interaction with the Katzes started to wear off as the conversation continued. "Our press conference is at one in the afternoon on Thursday in Sydney."

"So, that's eight, nine, ten o'clock tonight, right?"

"Did you have to start with the West Coast and count up?" Betsy teased.

"Well, I lived there for a couple of years, so yes. There were a few things I spoke with Ania about, so I had to convert the time often. I always added seven hours, then subtracted twelve because of America's twelve hours versus twenty-four hours. Then added a day. But I had to add two more hours for the Central time zone. Did that make sense?"

"And I'm supposed to trust you in the kitchen baking? You're probably going to try to add vegemite to everything."

"Oh! Can we?"

"Gods above, no!"

Violet laughed. "Fine. You are so mean. What's the plan?"

"All I had for lunch was a slice of flourless chocolate cake."

"You really are mean unless you have a second piece for me."

"I don't. It was given to me by the baker in Oz." Betsy shook her head. "I can't imagine who named that town! It's ridiculous."

"So, it's just after three. We have almost eight hours. What were you thinking?"

"I'm going to make a sandwich, then contact Ania. If she's willing, maybe we can get a tour of Sydney and then have lunch or dinner, depending on the point of view, with her. Then, after the press conference, head back here ... if you want."

"I'd like that. Then, when you have your call with the other Pillars on Thursday afternoon, maybe I could listen in again."

"I don't really see a problem with that. Keeping you informed with what's going on doesn't seem like a bad idea."

"When do you want me over there?"

Betsy stood and headed toward the kitchen. "Whenever you want to show up. Just let me know if I'm making two sandwiches or one."

"Two. I'm starved."

They transported to Ania's place. She lived in a ranch home in a large open property, far from any neighbors. Her property was a thirty-minute drive from most things she needed but she loved her solitude. Like all the Pillars, she could transport anywhere she needed to go when she wanted to get away.

"You know, Betsy," Ania's green eyes twinkled, "as large as your place is, my piece of land is larger. You should let me have the ven. They'd like it here better."

The shock rocketed through Betsy. She'd been coveting the large moth-like creatures since she'd spent a year on Torville Station Number Six during her hundredth year of life. Now that she had the pair, there was no way she would give them up.

Violet saw the look on her face and laughed. "I can speak to Commander Firoza. She doesn't want to keep any of the babies. I know Viera loves them, but I'm sure I can secure a couple for you on their next trip back here."

Ania narrowed her eyes at the two of them. "Okay, I'll take you somewhere to eat that isn't known for food poisoning."

As Betsy chuckled, Violet blanched. She didn't know Ania's sense of humor as well as Betsy did.

They ended up at a steakhouse. Once they'd ordered, they all relaxed, enjoying each other's company. Violet sipped her wine. "I've always heard that Earth has at least five Pillars, though sometimes there are more."

Ania nodded. "Right."

"Well, I'm curious. Does that mean the Pillars marry each other?" Betsy nearly choked on her soda while Ania's eyes danced. "And are there any kids being planned?"

"Nothing like a softball question," Betsy mumbled.

Ania lifted her beer in salute. "Great question, mate." She took a big gulp of her drink. "As it goes, the gift of the magic gene is dominant. So, we don't need to partner with the limited number of family lines that have carried the heavy load of knowledge throughout the generations." At the end of her statement, Ania winked and bobbed her eyebrows.

Betsy sighed and shook her head. "Over the years, there have been several approaches. When a magical woman had no rights and ended up pregnant, she often tried to separate from the father before he taught the child something against what the Pillars wanted. Some of the female wizards faked their deaths, finding other wizard families to live with until they could strike out on their own again. Some wizards just hid the truth. It isn't as hard as you may think. If the spouse seemed able to handle the truth, they were taught ... well, just about everything. My mom kept our secret and reveled in everything I learned until she passed. She was in awe of technology, loving what we had and others didn't."

"This is one time I agreed with Gandalf, believe it or not." Ania shook her head. "Your dad took a huge risk letting your mom know about us. Germany in that day and age was not a safe place for knowledge."

"But they were in love." A warmth filled Betsy at the memory of her mom. Gods, she missed her some days. Though the image of the person who brought her into the world was mostly gone from memory all these years later.

"That said, right now, none of us have planned kids ... that I know of. Betsy, have you heard anything?"

Betsy shook her head. "Not from Zuza or the boys. I think Zuza would've told me. We've been good friends for years."

Sipping her beer, Ania asked, "Any other questions?"

"Actually, yeah. Why is it that only Betsy has to deal with that obnoxious department of **DICKS**?"

Eyes wide, Ania almost did a spit-take with her drink. "Gods above, woman!" Then she laughed. "You know it was Betsy and her dad who came up with the damn idea. Despite several of us thinking it would come to a horrible end, they went ahead and created the department." One of her brows rose. "And I wasn't wrong, was I? Look where we are now."

"Oh, please. This all would've happened decades ago if it weren't for what we did. The governments of the world have been monitoring space for years. It was only *because* of what Dad and I did that the rest of the planet didn't know about aliens and magic for this long, and you know it."

Violet held up her hands. "Ladies, please. This sounds like an old fight. The question isn't the department's inception, but why others haven't helped once it was up and running."

Ania's face hardened. "Marco and Kafi were too young at the start. Kafi was barely out of his nappies when the department was started, and his parents were running the school in Africa. Marco's mom was thinking about having a kid and was working on that. Zuza and I were busy doing our own things and, honestly, Betsy has never asked for help. It's always been her pet project."

"I guess." Betsy shrugged. "I mean, we all have our own areas of the world, and I've been focused on North America. For the better part of the last hundred or so years, the majority of the job has been downplaying the department to new people. It's only been in the last two or three years that things have been interesting. And each of us has had to work with different governments to help the refugees, so no one's been specifically in the New York office."

Violet nodded. "So you haven't been upset?"

"Not really. If any of us needs help, we all jump in." She placed her hand on Violet's knee under the table and squeezed. "We have monthly meetings to ensure we're always on top of any important happenings in the world. It's only now that we need to communicate more frequently. Once everyone ... you know, in the world, is caught up with everything, and the global tension drops, we should be able to drop back down to talking less frequently."

The server came with their food, and the conversation shifted to news on Oz, magic, and Xantay.

"I'm Jack Johnson, and I'd like to welcome Pillar Doeth and Pillar North, our guests here in Sydney, who are here to answer questions this week. They'd like to remind everyone that there's a website at the bottom of our broadcast and linked in the QR code that will lead you to recordings of previous press conferences, the itinerary of upcoming press conferences, and answers to common questions. Now, I give you, Pillar Betsy Doeth!"

His smile wasn't quite as bright as their presenter's last week, but what it lacked in shine, he made up for in pep, energy, and an amazing Australian accent.

"Hi, everyone. Before I answer any questions, I'd like to start by mentioning that Major North isn't a Pillar of Earth but rather a major from Abritos, the chanziian planet. Now, what questions can I answer?"

"How does magic work, and how can I secure my own invitation to a secret magic school?" The question got several giggles from around the room.

Overall, Betsy preferred this start of questioning over the previous week's. "Magic is something a person has within them. I draw from a well of power. There are different types of proficiencies, some more common than others. As for individual people on Earth, the potential is there. It may or may not be present in people. Those of us who use magic aren't sure why there are so few who can access our power on Earth, and if, now that the news is out, more of you will be able to find your power well. We do have a place on the website to contact us if you think you are using magic. We'd like to help train you. We don't want issues or confusion in new wizards."

An older woman with a large hat and a sneer stood. "Are you planning on gathering us up and putting us in one of those 'camps' you Americans so love?"

It took Betsy a moment to breathe and force her face not to react. "No, ma'am. We very much would rather people live their own lives, just do it safely. The idea of having more than five people on the planet who understand, can use, and eventually can teach magic excites all of us. Our planet has always had the fewest wizards of any galaxy we know of. We'd love to hit average, which is about ten to fifteen percent of the population. If you do the math, we predict a large number of people contacting us in the near future."

A young man wearing a Gandalf outfit lifted his staff. "Is it just waving your hands or a staff, or can a person—a *wizard*—cast spells with, like, eye of newt?"

"I am more than happy to get into the minutiae of magic, but is this the direction you all want to go in today?"

Someone in the back, whom Betsy couldn't see, yelled, "Just answer the nerd's question already."

Tilting her head, Betsy raised an eyebrow. "Yes, there are spells that can be cooked up as well as created from the magic within."

A middle-aged man with salt and pepper hair smirked at them. "Can the pretty lady next to you do any magic?"

Violet's smile widened, then she shifted to her natural being with a sigh. "No, sir. I am not a wizard. My people do have a natural ability to shift our appearance subtly, which is why we could come to Earth when the krottel invaded Abritos, but beyond that, I'm as magic-blind as most people of Earth."

"If you did that to scare me off, ma'am, I'm afraid you failed. I think you may be even more fetching in your natural state." He waved his phone in the air and mouthed, "Call me."

A woman in the front, who gave off journalist vibes, leaned forward. "You keep saying there are five magic users on Earth, but any of us who were at the first press conference saw the magical display from the audience. It's been edited out of the replay, but I know what I saw. How can you claim only five wizards when there are obviously more?"

Thank the Gods I've spent time in Oz. "Great question. What you saw was someone using the magic around them, kind of like the last question you heard. A group who've learned to mix spells. I've spoken with them hand have seen their abilities. I will not downplay what they can do. They are impressive. But they are witches mixing spells, not wizards using an innate power from within."

"So, they're not as good as you?" the woman persisted.

"I did not say that," Betsy said slowly and clearly. "The word different doesn't imply better or worse. Some of what they can do is fantastic. I'm hoping they can create things my magic can't. The combination of the two may be something that will give Earth its greatest advantage. I'm truly excited to learn how we can work the two magics together."

Jack Johnson stepped forward. "It sounds like you took your own advice when speaking to this group. Don't go into any situation acting like you know more than anyone else."

After that, there wasn't time for many more questions. It took almost another hour before Betsy and Violet could make it back to Wisconsin, at which point it was midnight local time. They fell into bed, exhausted from another long day.

When Betsy woke, she decided to try out the soap she'd gotten from Oz. *Let's see how refreshed this really makes me feel!*

It didn't take more than a few seconds with the shampoo and soap before Betsy felt like she'd gotten a full eight hours of sleep and her first cup of coffee.

For fuck's sake, do they imbue everything in that town?

With her newfound energy, Betsy headed back into the bedroom. She found Violet still asleep in bed, the sun sparkling off her skin like glitter. Crawling into bed, she kissed the other woman's neck. "Morning, sexy. I'm hungry for breakfast, and you're on my menu."

Rolling onto her back, Violet smiled, her eyes slowly opening. "Hmm, morning, my storm cloud."

Betsy leaned down to kiss Violet properly, lifting her shirt at the same time. She slipped it over the beauty's head, breaking the kiss, and then she dropped down, deciding she wanted to kiss every inch of the woman below her.

She made her way down Violet's neck, nipping and licking. Violet tasted like a sweet dessert. Betsy took her time when she got to the luscious breasts, large and full. Betsy dragged her tongue around each bosom, sucking first one and then the other into her mouth, flicking the tip before lightly scraping the nipple with her teeth.

Each side got the attention it deserved as, below her, Violet quivered, moaning her delight.

Betsy enjoyed taking her time. Violet bent her knee between Betsy's legs, rubbing her thigh against Betsy's most sensitive area. Heat blossomed within her as she trailed her tongue down Violet's perfect abs.

She pulled Violet's shorts down as she went, then, once she was naked, returned her hands under Violet's luscious ass, squeezing and lifting. Violet groaned as Betsy licked up her center, flicking her tongue over Violet's clit. She'd wanted to taste this beautiful alien for weeks. Leaning in, Betsy buried her face into Violet, sucking and lapping up the slickness of her enjoyment.

With one hand, she stroked one finger deep within her before sliding in two fingers, probing in and out, twisting her hand to hit more sensitive spots.

Her mouth moved faster, as did her hand. Beneath her, Violet arched up, panting. Then she screamed, drenching Betsy's fingers with her orgasm. Betsy continued to move her fingers in and out, prolonging Violet's pleasure until her moans shifted to rough breaths and whimpers.

After a final kiss to her lower belly, Betsy crawled up to cuddle, wrapping her arms around the other woman.

Violet smiled, breathing roughly, then laughed. "I don't know if I can walk any time soon."

"That's okay. We have until after lunch. We have all morning to stay in bed and play."

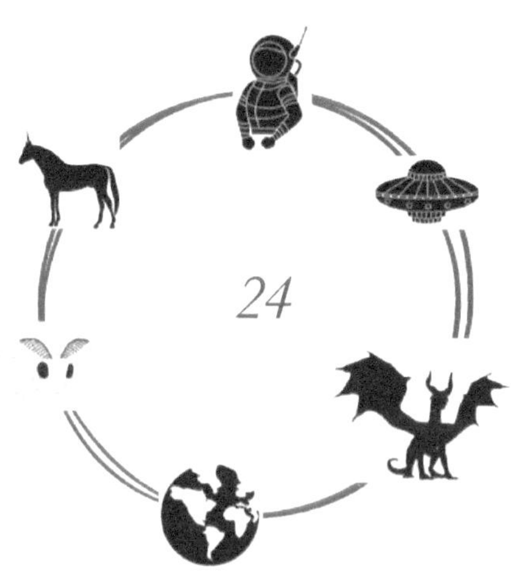

A Whole New World

Viera

Eyes shut, Viera felt sweat dripping down her hairline and back. The damn stones pinged off her radar like fire ants. "Seventeen."

"Excellent, Ms. Kor. I think we're done for today. You're getting better with these exercises. I'll be switching up our lessons." Flower Prancer turned and started walking toward downtown

Roxillion. He'd found a building that worked for him during his stay on-planet. No one was sure how long that'd be.

When he was out of sight, Viera turned to Horax, her guide back to Thorn's place. They'd only been on Abritos a few days, and she still didn't know her way around. "Did he just compliment me?"

The qynad rumbled in his gut, his version of a hearty laugh. "I believe so."

"But ... I ..." She stopped, uncertain what to say next.

"Trust me, Viera. I'm as dumbfounded as you."

They continued to walk in silence for a bit. The training spot was about a twenty-minute walk from town. It was selected so they could train some of the more explosive magics without having to worry about harming any of the homes or businesses.

Since landing, Viera had started training with Flower Prancer in the morning, having lunch with Scout, and then working on learning Galactic Standard in the afternoon. She'd wanted to learn the chanziian language but found it wasn't used much on-planet. Most of the beings knew it, but it was their second language ... or third. Because of business and off-world travel, Galactic Standard had taken over years earlier as a more important language for the population.

Above them, flying through the clouds, were a smattering of colorful birds. "Those are r'grazz, right? Birds?"

Horax looked, then grunted. "Yep. I see r'taffa and r'mast up there. The first are the multicolored birds we saw on our last trip out here."

"Oh, they are emitting a lot of joy." It was times like this that Viera enjoyed her proficiency in sensing.

"Their young must have just hatched." He jerked his head to the right. "The red ones, the ones that look a bit like the robins back on Earth, are r'mast."

As she watched, one of the r'mast dove, landing on a small brown rodent. It looked to be a mouse-type creature, but like several of the chanziian animals, it had six legs. "Wow, nature. Large, live, and totally real in a confusingly new way."

Amusement rolled off Horax. "That brown beast is a tor'hat."

She wasn't sure why the bird attacking the tor'hat was funny, but Horax wasn't usually callous.

She'd give him the benefit of the doubt. But then, as she watched, the tor'hat grew and changed from a dark brown to a construction-cone orange. The new creature looked more like a six-legged rat than a mouse, and Viera's heart beat faster. "Whoa!"

"Yep. It isn't only the chanziian who shapeshift on this planet, but the show isn't over, dear teacher." He pointed with a sharp claw.

The small red r'mast, so like a robin, quivered, then grew, just like the tor'hat. The feathers turned a deep navy blue as the bird morphed into something fierce and large, closer to the size of a hawk. Without any trouble at all, it picked up the tor'hat and flew off.

"Holy ... how many animals can do that on this planet?"

"No idea. Ask the boy. Scout tends to know a lot. He loves to read and retains everything. If anyone will one day take over the world, it's him."

Viera chuckled at that. Horax wasn't wrong. "Speaking of books, I keep hoping one of the boxes we empty will have books, but we keep opening boxes with useless items."

"Oh? What did you drag from Earth that you no longer want?" He perked up, sounding interested.

"Silly stuff."

"Tell me."

"Fine. I have a bunch of kitchen paraphernalia that is useless here. I should've left it back home. There isn't anything I can do with it."

"What sort of stuff?" Horax always paid close attention to any conversation he was in. He made the other person feel important.

Viera shrugged. "Mostly plates and silverware. I have my grandma's old collection of decorative spoons from around the world ... well, Earth. Silly, I know."

"Anything else?" He sounded genuinely interested. *Horax is such a great friend.*

"Don't laugh, but pillows. I didn't bring any furniture, but I had all these decorative pillows on my couches back home. I just boxed them up and brought them. The decision to come here, to pack up and follow Thorn, was so quick that I didn't critically think about anything. I think I have four or five boxes of pillows, both used and ones I had in storage for different holidays."

"Oh?" He seemed to perk up. "You know, if you want, I could take the pillows and spoons … well, all the kitchen supplies. I have plenty of storage space. I'm sure I can find a great home for all of the items … if you really don't want them."

"Are you sure? I don't want you to take the junk if it's going to be a burde—"

"No burden." He rumbled a laugh again. "Not a problem at all. Just put the boxes in the living room and let me know when to collect them." He almost purred the request.

Thank goodness for good friends.

They'd reached the door, and Viera smiled. "Thank you so much. I hated having all the boxes cluttering up Thorn's home. I'll have Scout help me. We'll give you a call in the next hour or so."

"Sounds good." His eyes almost shone. *I never realized how much he likes helping others.*

Scout was more than happy to help her gather the items they wouldn't need and stack them in the living room. "But first, I'm hungry. What should we have for lunch?"

"I could try making pasta."

He scrunched his nose. "Do you know how to use our kitchen, Ms. Kor?"

"Well, I have to learn eventually, right?"

"I guess." He didn't sound convinced.

Once she had the water boiling and the sauce simmering, they gathered the boxes for Horax. Just as they were about to contact him, a plume of black smoke wafted from the kitchen.

Laughing, Scout said, "Good thing you're going to be teaching and not cooking, Ms. Kor."

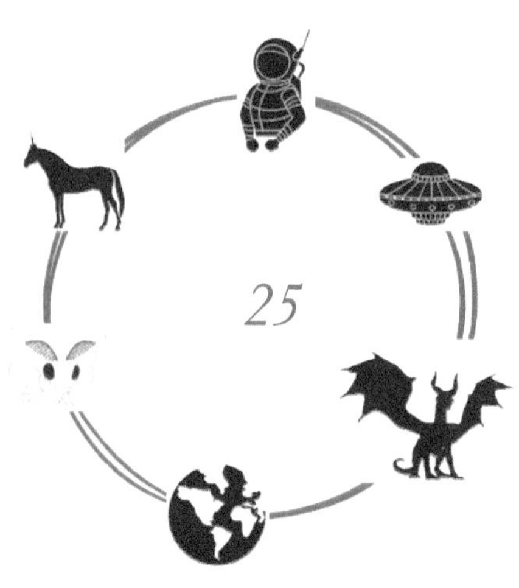

25

The Devil Made Me Do It

Betsy

The ven zoomed around the small office. When Betsy tried to let them out, they refused. Apparently, they wanted time with their staff, not freedom from the confines of the house.

Once she shut the door, the rascal Wes landed on her shoulder. He was almost too big, and

Buttercup respectfully perched next to Violet on the couch, vibrating and making happy sounds.

The meeting started at three, and the image of Ania narrowed her eyes at Betsy. "Don't let Violet forget her promise. I want a pair of ven flying around my house too, Pillar Doeth."

Marco and Kafi started squabbling about their desire for pets as well, and Betsy rubbed her temples. "Do you see what you've done? You had to demand it in front of the kids, didn't you?"

Ania laughed. "It's your own damn fault, parading your babies in front of us like some queen with her prizes."

"You think I have any control over where Wes ends up on my estate? Oh, I can't wait for you to have one of these devils. They're wonderful but completely uncontrollable."

Zuza whistled. "Children! Enough. For the record, I do not want one of those critters. I don't think it would fare well in my English apartment." He paused, one eyebrow raised, waiting for any other comments. When none came, he gave a curt nod. "Very good. Now, it's late here. I'm going to get this meeting started. Several people have stepped forward stating they think they have magic."

Betsy shook her head. "Did they come sign up on our website? I didn't receive any emails or notifications."

"No." Zuza sounded pissed. "They went to the local university following the request for volunteers for their research. From what I've heard, these people decided an English-run program would be preferable to an American government-sanctioned ... well, anything."

Anger swelled in Betsy, but she bit it back. "So, how many people have gone to university?"

"So far, three that I know of, but there could be more. I only know of these people because I have a friend in the police department here in town. Their families or friends all individually reported the volunteers missing, stating this program as the last place they were known to have been. In one case, a friend had even dropped her 'bestie' off there."

"Is the program really that widely known about?" Marco asked.

"Yeah, there are flyers all over town, especially in the pubs, about the university research. It pays well."

"Of course it does," Ania mocked. "It's a new toy, and everyone knows universities have all the funds."

That got everyone chuckling.

"Right," Zuza continued. "Well, the potential wizards have disappeared. There has been no contact via their mobiles or on social media. When the university was contacted, they said they hadn't heard of the three recruits. Actually, they mournfully admitted to no volunteers so far."

Kafi shook his head. "They're lying."

Nodding in agreement, Zuza continued, "That's our guess. But right now, there isn't anywhere to check. The university has opened all the labs. The phones are untraceable. My assumption is they've been turned off or destroyed."

"Well, fuck." Betsy wanted to go and find these people, but they needed more information to figure out where to look. "Any news on the religious crazies?"

"Here in Aussie, besides the devil finder I told you about last time, we have a very vocal female leader who has told her followers that if she can heal them, it's proof they have God on their side. If not, the devil rides them."

Kafi snorted. "I have a devil finder in Africa as well. He states he's finding the sinners. For a fee, he'll visit a village and cleanse it."

Zuza paled. "How many deaths are we talking about?"

"Too many, and because it's for religion, no one is stopping him."

Betsy felt queasy. "Okay, we each have to make sure our proper authorities know. This is getting out of hand. My department can't help what's happening in your region, Kafi, but it has to stop."

"Agreed. But if we bring more attention to it, I fear what public opinion will be."

They continued discussing possible directions to take.

If only there were a way to turn magic off as well as opening it up in people. But they weren't the magic police. They were just people with information.

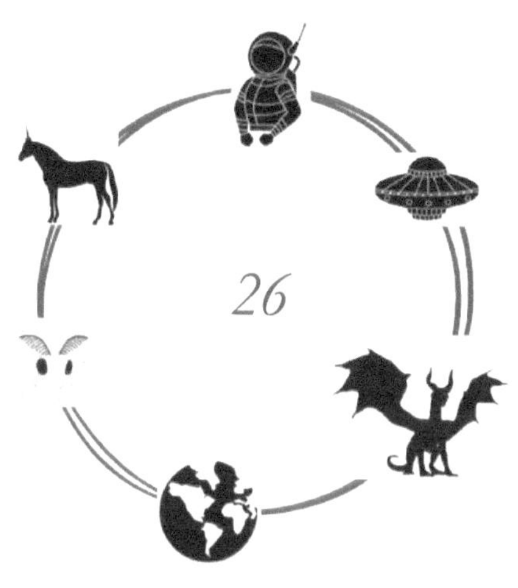

26

An Unexpected Guest

Betsy

Violet lay on top of Betsy, kissing and sucking her neck. Their legs were intertwined. Circling her hips, Violet rubbed her clit against Betsy's, grinding down. Under her, Betsy rolled her hips while grasping the other woman's shapely ass.

Betsy surged up, their bodies pushing together. A tiny thrill spiked through her at the feel of Violet's breasts pressed against her own. The slickness from both of them combined as they continued to gyrate their hips, sliding against each other.

"God," Violet panted in her ear. "I want to lick up every inch of you."

With a smirk, Betsy twisted and got Violet onto her back. The other woman squealed on the way down, followed by a small laugh. "You asked for it now."

"Oh?"

Flipping around, Betsy straddled Violet, dipping her head to feast on her drenched bits. Strong hands wrapped around her hips, lowering her down. As Betsy licked and sucked, she felt a similar play on her.

Then Violet pushed a finger into her while her other hand circled lower. She squawked, her mouth gagged by Violet's body. Then she felt laughter vibrate up through her.

Heat built in Betsy as they both continued. She trembled as she tried to focus on pleasuring Violet.

Then Violet did something with her hands and fireworks erupted in Betsy's head. She shook and tried to breathe. Small mews escaped her to Violet's most private parts as her mouth still worked at lapping up Violet's juices.

Beneath her, Violet tensed, and finally, Betsy rolled to the side, landing on her back, a quivering mass of joy. "Gods above, why do I have to go to that town and meet with those people? Why can't I just stay with you today? It's Saturday."

"Because you're a beautiful, smart, responsible person. Now go help that little girl."

Betsy sighed. "You're right." Rolling to her hands and knees, she found Violet's mouth and gave her a gentle kiss. "Will you be here when I get home?"

"I have some work to do at home, but you could come there. I could make ... or buy"—she smiled—"dinner."

"Sounds perfect."

Closing her eyes, Betsy focused on Pearl and pushed her intention through the jade Devlin had imbued for her: '*I should be near the school in five minutes.*'

She and Violet had just finished eating breakfast sandwiches, and the chanziian was already at the panel dialing up her home.

Betsy watched the stone, unsure what was supposed to happen or if she'd even used it correctly. "I feel like an idiot," she mumbled.

"But you're amazing," Violet said as she shimmered away.

Just when she was about to give up, the stone warmed slightly, and Pearl's voice spoke in her head: '*Sounds perfect. I'm already here with Dulaine. She was so excited she couldn't decide what she wanted to do—run around or draw. Mom and Dad will be here soon.*'

Shocked it worked, Betsy chuckled, slipped the stone in her pocket, and then tapped on the panel, telling it where she wanted to go. Her kitchen melted around her, and a moment later, she stood in a field.

Though it was early, the humidity was thick. Betsy quickly walked to the school, slipping into the cool air conditioning. Mr. and Mrs. Katz had beat her to the room. She'd asked Xantay to come later, after she'd had a moment to speak with the family.

"Good morning, Mrs. and Mr. Katz. I'm really glad we have this time to talk." The couple spoke with Pearl by the teacher's desk, watching Dulaine. Betsy walked up to them, the best smile she could manage on her face.

"Is that dragon here?" Mrs. Katz snapped at her.

We need to stay on good terms with these people. Too much is happening in the world ... we need help. "The qynad, Xantay? No. I asked her to come after I called for her." She took a deep breath. "I hoped to discuss an alliance between the Pillars and your town."

The mayor's face, if anything, got tighter. "What are you asking, Pillar Doeth?"

Betsy sighed. "Can we go back to you calling me Betsy?"

"I'll think about it. Now answer my question."

"Right. Well, everyone in your town knows about magic. I'm guessing Pearl explained how what you do differs from how we use our abilities, but it's still fantastic. The problem we're facing is we have an entire planet of people suddenly learning about aliens and the arcane. Their literal world has turned upside down."

Ms. Katz's eyes narrowed. "I don't see what that has to do with us. From what I understand, your people worked hard to keep our identity hidden, for which I thank you. Wouldn't working with you undo all of that?"

Betsy nodded, knowing her fears were real. "Right now, I'm the face of all magic wielders on Earth. I am one of five Pillars. The other four haven't been named or seen." She gazed into the eyes of each of the three members of the Katz family standing before her. "My goal is to help people who are discovering the arcane for the first time, not add another face to the public. I understand privacy and don't want to endanger you or anyone in this town. At the end of the day, we need more people. More help from people who know about the different powers when new magic users come forward. I fear the five of us won't be enough."

"You'll understand ... Betsy," she said the name with a bit of hesitation, "that I'll need some time to think about this. I also want to speak with the other leaders of the town."

"I can respect that." A weight lifted from Betsy. At least she hadn't said no, flat out.

"Now that you've registered your request—"

"Who is that?" Mr. Katz interrupted his wife, his brow creased. "Did you bring a boy with you to play with Dulaine? Do you have kids?"

Fear and apprehension filled Betsy as she slowly turned. *What kid would sneak into this school today?*

Sitting next to the young girl wasn't a boy. It wasn't even an Earthling. Betsy swallowed her frustration. "Elder Balzeno, to what do we owe the honor of your presence today?"

The dwarf looked up and smiled wide. "Pillar Doeth, you do an old dwarf honor by seeing past my seeming. So very few can. I came after speaking with Wizard Kor, former Pillar of Earth, newest wizard of Abritos ... one of their first, did you know that? With their inherent shape-shifting ability, that planet doesn't have many who can do more with manipulating the well of power from within."

His grin was infectious, and Betsy found herself smiling back. "I understand you learned of our humble town, but that doesn't explain why you are sitting and coloring with the child."

Eyes wide, Elder Balzeno stood and bowed. "I fear the Earthlings behind you look confused, Pillar Doeth."

Betsy gazed at the Katzes, then swore under her breath. "Did you bring the earpieces I gave you the other day?"

It appeared to take some effort for the three to tear their gaped-mouthed gazes from Elder Balzeno to Betsy. Mr. Katz shook his head and appeared focused first. "Mine are in my pocket. You said we needed them to speak with the dragon."

"The qynad."

"Oh, right, yes," he stammered.

Pearl kept looking back and forth between Betsy and Elder Balzeno. "You were speaking English, but he spoke ... I don't know. It didn't make sense."

"Put the earpiece in, and I'll introduce you." Betsy kept her voice light and calm. At the table, Dulaine giggled. Betsy could see she had her translator securely in place.

Pearl got hers in the quickest, then squatted next to her sister. "What's so funny, Du-Drop?"

"Balzeno. He's been asking me questions, and then he touched my forehead, and it tickled. It was funny."

"What did you find out?" A chill ran down her back. Dwarves were an odd bunch.

He sat back down. "Can you show me your necklace, Dulaine?"

Her eyes and mouth widened to cartoonishly large circles. "How did you know about that?"

Elder Balzeno continued to gaze at her until she pulled it off and handed it to him. Leaning forward, Betsy gasped. "My necklace. That was ... I ... Star Dancer gave that to me years ago."

"Then how does this girl have it, Pillar?" Elder Balzeno's voice was no longer light.

"He said it was to gather magic for my trips off-world. It felt heavy ... full. I took it off before its magic morphed. When I went to find it in my box, it was gone." Betsy searched the faces of the people in the small school.

"So, you lost it. A dwarven-imbued gift." His face hardened, eyes almost glowing. "Do you not value that which was given to you by an Elder?"

"Excuse me ..." Mrs. Katz tried to cut in.

"No." Balzeno held up a hand. "I am speaking to Pillar Doeth about respect." He turned back to face her. "I am displeased with how you treated one of my trinkets, Pillar Doeth. Time, care, and thought went into that gift."

"Just one moment?" Mrs. Katz continued, her spine stiff with determination.

"I am an Elder. Well over a thousand of your Earth years, possibly two ... I have yet to do the conversions. Let me speak with the youngling, Pillar Doeth, about this matter."

"But ..." Mrs. Katz lifted her hand as if she were a student in the class. "If I may. Just one thing. Please."

Both Betsy and Elder Balzeno snapped their gazes to her. The woman had moxie. Finally, he nodded slowly. "Of course, mother of Dulaine, wizard of Earth. I apologize. Say your piece."

Betsy slowly closed her mouth after it began to drop open. *Wizard?*

"I have a diary from one of my ancestors. She writes about Betsy and this Star Dancer ... was he really a talking horse?"

"A yonat, but you'll learn." Balzeno spoke gently to her.

"Okay, right, like the dragon—"

"Qynad." This time, Balzeno's voice was harder. "You've been reminded a few times. It's rude to not even try."

"Understood." Betsy saw the other woman's hands tremble. "Anyway, in this journal, my ancestor started following Betsy around. She was very good with see-me-not spells. One day, when Betsy wasn't around, she stole a necklace ... um, that necklace. She wanted to figure out how it worked. It's been passed down to the youngest in each generation ever since."

Balzeno shot Betsy a narrow look. "Was this the timeframe you started learning about wards and keeping your home secure?"

She smiled warily. "Yes. Before that, no one entered my home. But since then, no one can find it *to* enter."

Balzeno held up the pendant, letting the sun glint off it. There was a five-petaled rose quartz daisy within a circle of silver, molded in the shape of one of the GPS portals.

"Pillar Doeth, we will speak more about your care of Elder-made gifts ... but later. Now isn't the time. You were correct that if the magic in the pendant wasn't used, the pendant would alter its own purpose." He faced Mrs. Katz. "When this was yours, did you wear it every day?"

"No. It's pretty, but it mostly stayed in my jewelry box."

He nodded. "And you, young one." Balzeno tapped Dulaine's nose. "How often do you wear this pretty piece of jewelry?"

Excitement filled her face. "It's my favorite ... my good luck charm. I like wearing it every day. It feels like a shield of protection for me."

"Ah, intent." He sighed. "Mrs. Katz—"

"Please call me Vicky and my husband Porter."

"Vicky, your daughter has worn this necklace to the point that it has begun storing magic within her." He held up a hand, halting any comments. "It read her need for a shield. Your daughter ... is a marvel."

Vicky shook her head. "She's a magical dud, Elder Balzeno. The only one in town who can't light a candle."

A laugh barked out of him. "Of course she can't light a flame. Her proficiency isn't energy. It's liquid. Have you asked her to manipulate water?"

Betsy narrowed her eyes at Dulaine. "Do you know her second proficiency?"

"Of course she can imbue, just like everyone else in town." He tilted his head. "No, not like the others, like me."

"She's an actual magical imbuer?" The shock rocked Betsy. "The magic is within her, not manipulated from around?"

"Yes, but there's more." A chill ran down Betsy's spine. How could there be more? Wasn't a pendant that turned a girl into a wizard enough? "Does Dulaine have a favorite shirt? Maybe one she's recently outgrown?"

Pearl nodded. "I know just the one. The one with the rainbow-haired unicorn."

Porter nodded. "I can get it."

"Good. Let's all meet in the field."

It didn't take long for everyone to be there. Balzeno strung the shirt up on a branch of a tree. "Betsy, shoot an arrow at that shirt."

"It'll be magical." She was beginning to understand what Dulaine had done with the pendant.

"I know. But the family needs to understand."

She formed an arrow from dirt and stone and shot it at the shirt. It absorbed the impact, breaking up the magic.

The family gasped.

Vicky asked in a shaky voice, "What just happened?"

"Your daughter wanted a shield from the magic around her. She forced the pendant to change to what it did." Balzeno shrugged. "All my imbued items tend to have their own opinions."

Porter whistled. "That's amazing. She's created her own armor."

"No," Betsy said sternly. "You don't understand. Do you have a regular bow and arrow? Or some sort of weapon?"

"We need something or someone that can't be hurt by fire," Balzeno mumbled softly, gazing around the field.

Betsy and Balzeno said "Xantay" simultaneously.

It didn't take long for the qynad to shimmer in. Her eyes lit up when she saw everyone. "Balzeno! Dulaine! Betsy!"

Well, at least I'm on her list.

Balzeno explained what they wanted and the hazards involved.

Xantay nodded. Everyone else stepped back. The qynad stabbed the shirt, right through the center of the colorful unicorn, and the shirt exploded.

273

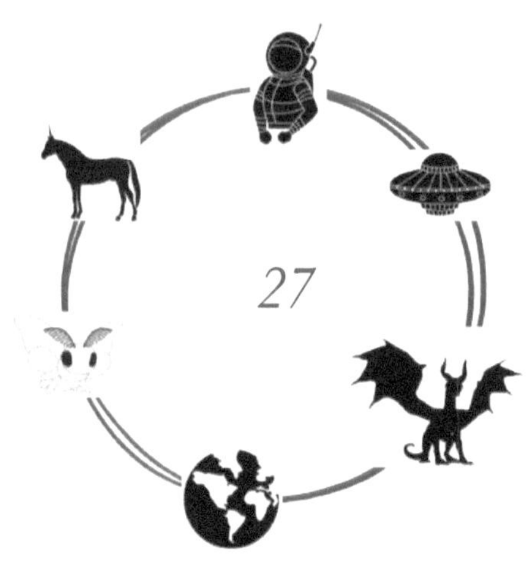

A Decision Made

Pearl

The giant red drag—qynad—*I will get this correct, even in my head!*—slammed her body down on the fire before it could get out of hand. Pearl gazed at her hands, watching as they trembled. "Will all her clothes do that?"

Balzeno's head rocked from left to right like a bobblehead. His long beard looked like the pole supporting it. Pearl tried not to react to her own thoughts. He said, "I can figure out a way to undo the weavings worked into the material. It shouldn't take long."

Mom licked her lips. "You said our daughter was a wizard, like the Pillars. That means she'll use magic like them, not us. Should we send her somewhere to be trained? Can we go with her? She's never been away from us."

"No," both Betsy and the dwarf said.

Betsy signaled the dwarf to speak. "She shouldn't be separated from her family. I'm sure Pillar Doeth or one of the other Pillars can come in and train her once every ..."

"Week or so," Betsy provided. "She'll have plenty of time to study and learn."

"Right you are, Pillar Doeth. Wizard Dulaine should spend most of her time being a kid." He spun on his heel. It amused Pearl that someone just shorter than her sister had such a large bearing. Everyone felt it. Even Mom gave him respect because of how much force he seemed to give off. "Once I've returned home to get some of my affairs in order, I would like to arrange to spend some time as a liaison to Earth."

For the first time ever, Pearl saw a reaction on Betsy's face. Her jaw actually dropped. Then she shook herself, composing herself back to a neutral expression. "I didn't think the dwarves had liaisons, Elder Balzeno."

"We do with new planets. Now that Earth has opened, I feel you are in need of our ... guidance. I will not have the yonats as the only Elder race to help direct your world."

The smile that spread across Betsy's face was blinding. "We would be honored to have you, Elder. Let me know where you'd like to live, and I'll personally make sure the accommodations are to your liking."

"Why, I thought it'd be obvious. I would like to live here. Part of my plan is to ensure young Wizard Dulaine has proper tutelage in the use of imbuing." He gazed at her with pride. "It has been so long since we've had new wizards with this proficiency."

Mom shimmied slightly, then plastered on her own welcoming smile. "I will have everything in order by the time you return. There is a house on our block we can set up for you."

"Hmm." He searched the woods behind the school. "Pillar Doeth, I'd like something like what you have built out there." He pointed.

"Do you know what I have?"

His look was flat.

Betsy shut her eyes and nodded. "That will take a couple of months. There isn't ... anything ... out here now. You should take Vicky up on her offer while we get your new home built."

"Excellent. Now, I think we're done here. Is there anything—"

"Oh! You're still here." Devlin came running into the field, his eyes wild.

Mom turned to him. "Devlin? Do you need something?"

"I figured it out. I think. But we need to test it. I've spent the last two days experimenting and spelling and—"

Dad put a hand on Devlin's forehead. "Have you slept or eaten?"

"What? Yeah ... I mean, I think so?"

Pearl sighed. Worry for her friend battled with her interest in his latest creation. "Okay, Dev, what have you done?"

He held up a three-inch wide leather band, about six feet long, with a smooth sky-blue-and-black stone the size of a small tangerine secured in the center.

Balzeno squinted at the creation, then slowly lifted his hand, stroking down until he touched the gem. "Is this chrysocolla?"

With a bit of a freaked-out expression, Devlin searched the faces of everyone in the field. He finally nodded quickly. "Yeah. That's what it is."

"Brilliant. It looks sound. And you came up with this on your own?"

"Um, yes? Do you know what it is? I'm Devlin, by the way."

"Ah, sorry, Elder Balzeno. Dwarf."

A small laugh huffed out of Devlin. "Sorry, um, I'm human."

One side of Balzenos mouth turned up. "Thank you for the information, Devlin, Witch of Earth." He bowed his head. "Shall we test this out?"

"Oh, yes." Devlin seemed just as confused as the rest, even though he'd brought the contraption.

Balzeno turned to Betsy. "Pillar Doeth, if you would please secure this to Xantay's neck. The rest of you, please remove your earpieces for a test."

What did Devlin do? What is going on? And how did Balzeno know? I know he's an Elder ... and old, but what is happening? Pearl reached up and took the earpiece out. She watched as everyone but Betsy did the same. Betsy was busy securing the leather belt around the qynad's neck.

Once it was on, Belzeno adjusted where the gem lay against the skin. Scales? Fur? Body? Hide? What did you call the body of a qynad?

Balzeno smiled up at Xantay, then said ... something. She realized it was like what he'd said at the start. She couldn't understand him. Then the qynad opened her mouth and ... "I don't know, Elder, it feels strange having it around my neck. What's it supposed to do?"

Pearl's jaw dropped.

Devlin whooped. "It worked."

Balzeno smiled and tapped his ear. Pearl put her earpiece in and saw Devlin do the same. Then the dwarf said, "Have confidence in your work, youngling." He turned to Betsy. "Yes, I believe this is exactly where I need to be."

Pearl braced herself, then turned to her parents. "Mom, Dad, I want to work with the Pillars. If Du-Drop is a wizard, if she has magic like them, not us,

I want to understand everything I can. In the end, she's one of us, and we take care of our own."

28

We Have a Problem

Betsy

On Monday morning, Betsy and Violet sat in the conference room, waiting for Juk to show up. They drank coffee and ate donuts from a box they'd brought in for the early meeting.

Juk rushed in, eyes wild. "I'm sorry I'm late, I just ... we have a problem."

Betsy slowly lifted her cup of coffee, leaning back in her seat. She couldn't imagine an issue beyond the ones she had brought to discuss with him. "Oh?"

"Look, I know you want to bring the, um, qynad, to the next press conference, but ... look, I tried to meet with her on Friday, and it didn't work." The man sounded frantic. His normal cocky attitude was nowhere to be seen.

She took a slow, deep breath, then released it. The scent of the coffee helped to relax her. "Okay, Juk, tell me, what happened? I saw Xantay on Saturday and she didn't mention anything." *Then again, with everything else, there wasn't much time to talk about Juk.*

Violet leaned forward, her head tilted. Betsy smiled as the sun lightened her blond hair. It had been a few days since she'd seen Violet's human persona, and she'd forgotten how much she liked both versions of her beauty.

With more patience than Betsy felt, Violet asked, "What exactly went wrong, Juk? Were you not able to get to a common meeting spot, or was the technology described too complicated ... because I'm sure we could help."

"What?" His eyes widened. "I don't understand what you're even saying." He leapt from his seat, pacing the length of the room. "I got to the island where she's been staying and ... God above, she's big. When we were on that ship ... but we were all in a room, and everyone spoke English. It never occurred to me to ask why or how, but everyone did."

Shutting her eyes, Betsy scrunched up her face, realization dawning on her. "Juk, did you wear the earpiece we gave you?"

He stopped mid-pace. "The one for my phone? I mean, thank you, but it doesn't work that well. I haven't been able to get it to connect."

She squeezed her hands until her nails bit into her palms. *I am not allowed to harm this imbecile.* "Juk, where is the earpiece now?"

Violet rubbed Betsy's arm, a smile on her face. "I mean, it's kind of funny, right? Can he dress himself? Or does he have help?"

Her question was so earnest that Betsy couldn't stop the laugh that bubbled out of her.

"It's on my dresser at home, why? Is it fixable?"

Betsy relaxed her hands before her nails drew blood, then picked up her coffee to take another sip. "Juk, what we gave you was a translator. If you had worn it on Friday, you could've spoken to Xantay. As it goes, we have another solution, so don't worry about it for her. However, there are other things we need to talk about."

"A what now?"

"It lets you hear English when aliens speak to you. A translator." Betsy wondered why it was harder to explain things to him than just about anyone else.

"Like a babelfish from *Hitchhiker's Guide to the Galaxy*?"

She smiled. "Something like that, yes." She selected a donut and threw it at him, hitting him in the center of his forehead. "If you'd read the damn files, *all* of them, things would go a lot smoother."

He slumped. "Do you know how many there are?"

"Yes. But this isn't the time to mess around. Aliens are coming, and we can't be caught with our asses hanging out."

"Aliens?"

"Yes. Xantay is only the second ... third ... maybe fourth of our liaisons if you count Violet, Flower Prancer, and possibly Toby."

"Toby?"

"The files, Juk. Read the fucking files."

"Okay, I will. I promise it will be all I do until they're fully integrated into my mind. But tell me, why won't I need the earpiece the next time I meet Xantay? Or is that any of the liaisons?"

Betsy spent some time filling him in on Oz, their magic, and the collar Devlin had made. After that, they discussed what the Pillars had found out.

"I haven't heard about any religious crazies in the US. I don't know if we can do much in the other countries."

"What about the missing people?" Violet asked. "That's within the universities."

"It's still on foreign soil. You said it was three people?" Juk took detailed notes as they spoke.

Betsy pulled out her phone. "Let me call Zuza and confirm with him." She shot off a text and quickly received an update.

"It's up to seven missing people. No trail on any of them."

It was Juk's turn to get a pained look on his face. "We still face the issue of imposing US rule over there. I can send out feelers with the British government, but again, there isn't a lot of direct action we can do beyond offering our help."

Betsy nodded. "I figured. Can you see if there's anything like this happening here? If self-proclaimed magic users are disappearing there, I'm guessing it's happening in other places."

"That, I can do. I'll also see if we can increase the amount of information we're allowed to share."

"Good. Thank you." It was the first time she'd felt something going right in one of these meetings. Apparently, there were some areas of his job he could do.

"Is there anything else?"

"Two more items. First, one of the dwarves will be moving to Oz as a trainer and liaison."

The color drained from Juk's face. "Aren't the dwarves"—his voice lowered as if speaking too loud would bring bad things ... or maybe one of the dwarves themselves to the meeting—"Elders?"

Betsy laughed. "Yes, they are. But they're also the best resource we have on imbuing magic. If Elder Balzeno is willing to come, I, for one, will cheer."

"Okay, what do we need to do?"

"He has some requests for living arrangements. I'll email them to you. They are extensive but important. If the government can't afford everything, the Pillars can. There is no 'no' in this list."

"Okay, got it." Juk nodded. "I'm guessing we can afford the majority of anything he requests. What's the second item?"

"Pearl Katz will be joining my team. We need more magic users to help with information gathering and dissemination. She'll come to Wisconsin on Friday. We offered to transport her, but she's afraid of how technology will mix with her form of magic. So, for now, she and Cassidy, her best friend, will be driving north."

Juk smiled. "Two young women. I wish you all the luck with that."

"Thank you. Though I may transport them while they sleep to get to our different engagements. Driving to Dubai, or rather the press conference after that, doesn't sound feasible."

"No, it doesn't."

As the meeting ended, Betsy felt cautiously optimistic.

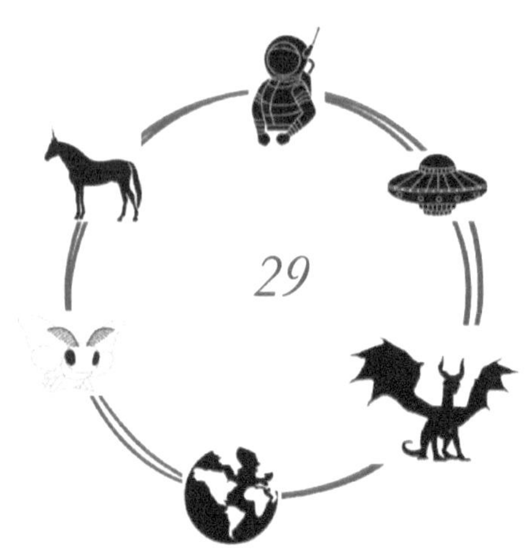

29

Didn't Mean to Step on Your Toes

Betsy

The server placed calamari on the table between Betsy and Violet. "Enjoy. Do you need anything else? More water, wine, bread?"

Betsy smiled. "No, thank you. This will be great."

"Wonderful. Your meals will be ready in about ten minutes." He spun on his heel, the shine on his shoes catching the light from the myriad of candles around the room.

Violet watched him disappear behind a wall. "They're all so ... tidy."

"I mean, on the ship, you all have your uniforms. Is this much different?"

"Yes! Our uniforms define rank. All of these people wear the same thing and are of the same rank."

Betsy leaned over to kiss her. "I am corrected, oh wise one. Now, let's enjoy the appetizer." She picked up the calamari and served some on each of their smaller plates. "Are you ready to see how everyone takes asking questions of Xantay?"

Violet's eyes danced. "Tomorrow is going to be fun. I don't know what will be more entertaining, the people asking questions or Xantay's pure excitement at it all."

"I just hope that gem can keep up with the speed at which she speaks." Betsy slapped a hand over her mouth. "Do you realize the room will be full of translators, and whenever she speaks, her words will come out in their language. No one will know what's going on. It'll be the biggest scandal and topic of the day. It almost doesn't matter what we do. Between the qynad and the fact that every word she speaks is universally understood ... Gods above, we may as well sit back and drink cocktails."

Violet snorted. "Can you imagine? No one will even care about us. We'll be old news."

Their entrées came, ribeye for Betsy and a New York strip for Violet. They focused on eating while the server refilled their wine.

As they debated dessert, Betsy's phone rang. She looked at the display. "It's Pearl. I can't imagine why she'd call."

"Answer it." Violet's voice brooked no argument.

"Are you sure?"

"Yes."

"Hello?" Betsy spoke low, trying not to disturb the tables around them.

"Betsy? Is that you?" Pearl sounded frantic.

"Yes. What's wrong?"

"It's Dulaine. She's gone."

"Slow down. What do you mean?" Betsy's heart started to beat harder.

"She headed up to bed to read. Then Dad tucked her in for bed. I was packing to drive to Wisconsin tomorrow. I wanted to give her one more hug before she turned off her lights. But her room was empty."

"And—"

"She's not in the house. I checked everywhere." Pearl's breath came over the line rough and haltingly.

"Okay, we'll be there as soon as we can." She wanted to tell Pearl that everything would be okay, but she couldn't. If one of the university science teams had taken her, who knew what they were doing.

She hung up and stood, tossing bills on the table. Violet's eyes widened. "That's a lot."

"It's fine. We need to go."

"What happened?"

"Someone took Dulaine. If those scientists think they can study a child under my care, they do *not* know who they've messed with. Not even an Elder will stop my wrath."

A chill went down her back as she realized how true the words were. Her anger fueled her magic, and the earth rumbled and rolled with the power that leaked from her. Around her, she heard the mumblings of people speaking about an earthquake.

"But we're in the Midwest. We're safe from such things."

Once outside, Betsy released her frustration, lifting her arms and screaming to the sky. The animalistic sound was a call to her ancestors, letting them know that Betsy Doeth was on the warpath. Even if no one else would stop these people, she would.

Once she finished, she doubled over, grasping her knees, breathing hard. Violet ran over to her. "Are you okay?"

"Yeah ... I'm ... yes. I just needed to make a pledge to myself to see this to the end."

"But, Betsy, not only did the ground shake but you were engulfed in what looked like a twister of wind. For several seconds, I couldn't see you." She rubbed Betsy's back. "Are you sure you're okay?"

Slowly standing, Betsy gazed at the leaves and twigs littered around her. "Yeah, I'm fine." She shook her head. "Wind? Like strong winds?"

"Yes."

"Huh, that's ... unexpected. But I'll worry about that later. Right now, we have a girl to find."

Thank you for reading!
Conflict Reawakened

Please Leave a review for this book so others know how much you enjoyed reading it.

Find more information on my <u>books on my website</u>

About the Author

Harlowe Frost has been a teacher at both the high school and college level. Her parents instilled a love of reading from a young age. She grew up in the queer community. Her favorite genre growing up was fantasy and science fiction, that is, until she discovered urban fantasy and paranormal romance. What she never found in those books was the diversity in background, gender identity, and sexuality she saw in the people around her. She decided if she couldn't find that in what she read, then she would write it herself. This started her writing paranormal romance with a LGBTQ+ background.